Daddy Was a Number Runner

Daddy Was a Number Runner

LOUISE MERIWETHER

FOREWORD BY JAMES BALDWIN
AFTERWORD BY NELLIE Y. McKAY

THE FEMINIST PRESS
AT THE CITY UNIVERSITY OF NEW YORK
NEW YORK CITY

Published in 2002 by the Feminist Press at the City University of New York
The Graduate Center, 365 Fifth Avenue, Suite 5406, New York, NY 10016

feministpress.org

First Feminist Press edition 1986
Originally published in 1970 by Prentice Hall

Brief portions of this work appeared, in different form, in *The Antioch Review*
and *Negro Digest*.

"Trouble in Mind," words and music by Richard M. Jones, © 1926, 1937 by
MCA Music, a division of MCA, Inc., New York. Copyright renewed. Used
by permission. All rights reserved.

("What Did I Do to Be So) Black and Blue," Harry Brooks, Andy Razaf, and
Thomas Waller, © 1929 by Mills Music, Inc. Copyright renewed. Used by
permission. All rights reserved.

Cover photo by Bill Hinton. Louise Meriwether Papers, 1968–2013, Stuart A.
Rose Manuscript Archives, Rare Book, and Archives Library.

Library of Congress Cataloging-in-Publication Data
Meriwether, Louise.
    Daddy was a number runner / Louise Meriether ; foreword by James
    Baldwin ; afterword by Nellie Y. McKay.
    p. ; cm. — (Contemporary classics by women series)
    I. Title.   II. Series
    PS3563.E738D3 2002   813'.54   86-9019
    ISBN 978-1-55861-442-7 (pbk.)

This novel was written with the assistance of a grant from
the Louis M. Rabinowitz Foundation.

No man is an island and so I pay my dues to the many people who have encouraged me, one way or another, during the evolution of this book. Thank you Catherine C. Hiatt, George Griffin, James Baldwin, Professor Joseph A. Brandt, The Watts Writers' Workshop, its founder Budd Schulberg and president Harry Dolan, the Altadena Writers' Workshop, Venia Martin, Junita Jackson

and

first, last and forever, my mother and my swinging family who have always loved me.

In memory of my father
Marion Lloyd Jenkins

Foreword by James Baldwin

I received a questionnaire the other day—democracy prides itself on its questionnaires, just as it is endlessly confirmed and misled by its public opinion polls—and the first question was, *Why do you continue to write?* Writers do not like this question, which they hear as *Why do you continue to breathe?* but sometimes one can almost answer it by pointing to the work of another writer. There! one says, triumphantly. Look! *That's* what it's about—to make one see—to lead us back to reality again.

The streets, tenements, fire-escapes, the elders, and the urgent concerns of childhood—or, rather, the helpless intensity of anguish with which one watches one's childhood disappear—are rendered very vividly indeed by Louise Meriwether, in her first novel, *Daddy Was a Number Runner.* We have seen this life from the point of view of a black boy growing into a menaced and probably brief manhood; I don't know that we have ever seen it from the point of view of a black girl on the edge of a terrifying womanhood. And the metaphor for this growing apprehension of the iron and insurmountable rigors of one's life are here conveyed by that game known in Harlem as the numbers, the game which contains the possibility of making a "hit"— the American dream in black-face, Horatio Alger revealed, the American success story with the price tag showing! Compare the heroine of this book—to say nothing of the landscape—with the heroine of *A Tree Grows in Brooklyn* and you will see to what extent poverty wears a color—and also, as we put it in Harlem, arrives at an *attitude.* By this time, the heroine of *Tree* (whose name was also Francie, if I remember correctly) is among those troubled Americans, that silent (!) majority which wonders what black Francie wants, and why she's so unreliable as a maid.

Shit, says Francie, sitting on the stoop as the book ends, looking outward at the land of the free, and trying, with one thin bony black hand to stem the blood which is beginning to rush from a nearly mortal wound. That monosyllable resounds all over this country, all over the world: it is a judgment on this civilization rendered the more implacable by being delivered by a child. The mortal wound is not physical, the book, so far from being a melodrama, is very brilliantly understated. The wound is the wound made upon the recognition that one is regarded as a worthless human being, and, further, in the case of this particular black girl, upon the recognition that the men, one's only hope, have also been cut down and cannot save you. Louise Meriwether wisely ends her book before confronting us with what it means to *jump the broomstick!*—to have a black man and a black woman jump over a broomstick is the way slave-masters laughingly married their slaves to each other, those same white people who now complain that black people have no morals. At the heart of this book, which gives it its force, is a child's growing sense of being one of the victims of a collective rape—for history, and especially and emphatically in the black-white arena, is not the past, it is the present. The great, vast, public, historical violation is also the present, private, unendurable insult, and the mighty force of these unnoticed violations spells doom for any civilization which pretends that the violations are not occurring or that they do not matter or that tomorrow is a lovely day. People cannot be, and, finally, will not be treated in this way. This book should be sent to the White House, and to our earnest Attorney General, and to everyone in this country able to read—which may, however, alas, be a most despairing statement. We love—the white Americans, I mean—the notion of the little woman behind the great man: perhaps one day, Louise Meriwether will give us *her* version of *What Every Woman Knows*.

Until that hoped for hour, because she has so truthfully conveyed what the world looks like from a black girl's point of view, she has told everyone who can read or feel what it means to be a black man or woman in this country. She has achieved an assessment, in a deliberately minor key, of a major tragedy. It is a considerable achievement, and I hope she simply keeps on keeping on.

PART I

DADDY
WAS A
NUMBER
RUNNER

ONE

"I dreamed about fish last night, Francie," Mrs. Mackey said, sliding back the chain and opening the door to admit me. "What number does Madame Zora's dream book give for fish?"

"I dreamed about fish last night, too," I said, excited. Maybe that number was gonna play today. "I dreamed a big catfish jumped off the plate and bit me. Madame Zora gives five fourteen for fish."

I smiled happily at Mrs. Mackey, ignoring the fact that if I stood here exchanging dreams with her, I'd be late getting back to school and Mrs. Oliver would keep me in again.

"What more hunch could a body want," Mrs. Mackey grinned, "us both dreaming about fish. Last night I dreamed I was going under the Bridge to buy some porgies and it started to rain. Not raindrops, Francie, but fish. Porgies. So I just opened up my shopping bag and caught me a bagful. Ain't that some dream?"

She laughed, her cheeks puffing up like black plums, and I laughed with her. You had to laugh with Mrs. Mackey, she was that jolly and fat. She waddled to the dining-room table and I couldn't keep my eyes off her bouncing, big behind. When she passed by in the street, the boys would holler, "Must be jelly 'cause jam don't shake," and she would laugh with them. They were right. Her behind was a quivering, shivering delight and I hoped when I grew up I would have enough meat on my skinny butt to shimmy like that.

Mrs. Mackey sat at the dining-room table and began writing her number slip.

"Mrs. Mackey," I said timidly, "my father asks would you please have your numbers ready when I get here so I won't have to wait. I'm always late getting back to school."

"They's ready, lil darlin'. I just wanna add five fourteen to my slip. I'm gonna play it for a quarter straight and sixty cents combination. How is your daddy and your mama, too?"

"They're both fine."

She handed me her number slip and two dollar bills which I slipped into my middy blouse pocket.

"Them's my last two dollars, Francie, so you bring me back a hit tonight, you hear? I didn't mean to spend so much but I couldn't play our fishy dreams cheap, right?"

We both giggled and I left. I raced down the stairs, holding my breath. Lord, but this hallway was funky, all of those Harlem smells bumping together. Garbage rotting in the dumbwaiter mingled with the smell of frying fish. Some drunk had vomited wine in one corner and peed in another, and a foulness oozing up from the basement meant a dead rat was down there somewhere.

The air outside wasn't much better. It was a hot, stifling day, June 2, 1934. The curbs were lined with garbage cans overflowing into the gutters, and a droopy horse pulling a vegetable wagon down the avenue had just deposited a steaming pile of manure in the middle of the street.

The sudden heat had emptied the tenements. Kids too young for school played on the sidewalks while their mamas leaned out of their windows searching for a cool breeze or sat for a moment on the fire escapes.

Knots of men, doping out their numbers, sat on the stoops or stood wide-legged in front of the storefronts, their black ribs shining through shirts limp with sweat. They spent most of their time playing the single action—betting on each number as it came out—and they stayed in the street all day until the last figure was out. I was glad Daddy was a number runner and not just hanging around the corners like these men. People were always asking me if I knew what number was out, like I was somebody special, and I guess I was. Everybody liked an honest runner like Daddy who paid off promptly the same night of the hit. A number runner is something like Santa Claus and any day you hit the number is Christmas.

I turned the corner and raced down forbidden 118th Street because I was late and didn't have time to go around the block. Daddy didn't want me in this street because of the prostitutes, but I knew all about them anyway. Sukie had told me and she ought to know. Her sister, China Doll, was a whore on this very same street. Anyway, it was too early for them to be out hustling, so Daddy didn't have to worry that I might see something I shouldn't.

A half-dozen boys standing in front of the drugstore were acting the fool, as usual, pretending they were razor fighting, their knickers hanging loose below their knees to look like long pants. Three of them were Ebony Earls, for sure, I thought. I tried to squeak past them but they saw me.

"Hey, skinny mama," one of them yelled. "When you put a little pork chops on those spareribs I'm gonna make love to you."

DADDY WAS A NUMBER RUNNER

The other boys folded up laughing and I scooted past, ignoring them. I always hated to pass a crowd of boys because they felt called upon to make some remark, usually nasty, especially now that I was almost twelve. So I was skinny and black and bad looking with my short hair and long neck and all that naked space in between. I looked just like a plucked chicken.

"Hey, there goes that yellow bastard," one of the boys yelled. They turned their attention away from me to a skinny light kid who took off like the Seventh Avenue Express when he saw them. With a wild whoop the gang lit out after him, running over everybody who didn't move out of their way.

"Damn tramps," a woman muttered, nursing her foot that had been trampled on.

I held my breath, hoping the light kid would escape. The howling boys rounded Lenox Avenue and their yells died down.

I ran down the street and turned the corner of Fifth Avenue, but ducked back when I saw Sukie playing hopscotch by herself in front of my house, not caring whether she was late for school or not. That Sukie. She was a year older than me, but much bigger. I waited until her back was turned to me, then with a burst of energy I ran toward my stoop. But she saw me and her moriney face turned pinker and she took out after me like a red witch. I was galloping around the first landing when I heard her below me in the vestibule.

"Ya gotta come downstairs sometime, ya bastard, and the first time I catch ya I'm gonna beat the shit out of ya."

That Sukie. We were best friends but she picked a fight whenever she felt evil, which was often, and if she said she was going to beat the shit out of me, that's just what she would do.

I kept on running until I reached the top floor and then I collapsed on the last step, leaning my head against the rusty iron railing. I heard someone on the stairs leading up to the roof and my heart began that crazy tap dancing it does when I get scared.

Somebody whispered: "Hey, little girl."

I tiptoed around the railing and peaked up into the face of that white man who had followed me to the movies last Monday. He had tried to feel my legs and I changed my seat. He found me and sat next to me again, giving me a dime. His hands fumbled under my skirt and when he got to the elastic in my bloomers, I moved again. It was the same man, all right, short and bald with a fringe of fuzzy hair around the back of his head. He was standing in the roof doorway.

"Come on up for a minute, little girl," he whispered.

I shook my head.

"I've got a dime for you."

"Throw it down."

"Come and get it. I won't hurt you. I just want you to touch this."

He fumbled with the front of his pants and took out his pee-pee. It certainly was ugly, purple and wet looking. Sukie said that everybody did it. Fucked. That's how babies were made, she said. I believed the whores did it but not my own mother and father. But Sukie insisted everybody did it, and she was usually right.

"Come on up, little girl. I won't hurt you."

"I don't wanna."

"I'll give you a dime."

"Throw it down."

"Come on up and get it."

"I'm gonna tell my Daddy."

He threw the dime down. I picked it up and the man disappeared through the roof door. I went back around the railing and leaned on our door and the lock sprang open. Daddy was always promising to fix that lock but he never did.

Our apartment was a railroad flat, each small room set flush in front of the other. The door opened into the dining room, so junky with heavy furniture that the room seemed tinier than it was. In the middle of the room a heavy, round mahogany table squatted on dragon-head legs. Against the wall was a long matching buffet with dragon heads on the sideboards. Scattered about were four straight-back chairs with the slats falling out, their tall backs also carved with ugly dragons. The furniture, scratched with scars, was a gift from the Jewish plumber downstairs, and was one year older than God.

"Mother," I yelled. "I'm home."

"Stop screaming, Francie," Mother said from the kitchen, "and put the numbers up."

I took the drawer out of the buffet, and reaching to the ledge on the side, pulled out an envelope filled with number slips. I put in Mrs. Mackey's numbers and the money, replaced the envelope on the ledge, and slid the drawer back on its runners. It stuck. I took it out again and shoved the envelope farther to the side. Now the drawer closed smoothly.

"Did you push that envelope way back so the drawer closes good?" Mother asked as I went into the kitchen.

"Yes, Mother."

I sat down at the chipped porcelain table, tilting crazily on uneven legs. Absentmindedly I knocked a scurrying roach off the table top to the floor and crunched it under my sneaker.

"If you don't stop racing up those stairs like that, one of these days you gonna drop dead."

"Yes, Mother."

I wanted to tell her that Sukie had promised to beat me up again, but Mother would only repeat that Sukie would stop bullying me when I stopped running away from her.

Mother was short and dumpy, her long breasts and wide hips all sort of running together. Her best feature was her skin, a smooth light brown, with a cluster of freckles over her nose. Her hair was short and thin, and she had rotting yellow teeth, what was left of them. In truth, she had more empty spaces in her mouth than she had teeth, but you would never know she was sensitive about it except for the fact that she seldom smiled. It was hard to know what Mother was sensitive about. Daddy shouted and cursed when he was mad, and danced around and hugged you when he was feeling good. But you just couldn't tell about Mother. She didn't curse you but she didn't kiss you either.

She placed a sandwich before me, potted meat stretched from here to yonder with mayonnaise, which I eyed with suspicion.

"I don't like potted meat."

"You don't like nothing. That's why you're so skinny. If you don't want it, don't eat it. There ain't nothing else."

She gave me a weak cup of tea.

"We got any sugar?"

"Borrow some from Mrs. Caldwell."

I got a chipped cup from the cupboard and going to the dining-room window, I knocked on our neighbor's window-pane. The Caldwells lived in the apartment building next door and our dining rooms faced each other. They were West Indians and Maude was my best friend, next to Sukie. We were the same age, but where my legs were long,

Maude's were bowed just like an O. Maude's father had died last year, and Pee Wee, her oldest brother, had just gone off to jail again, which was his second home. Maude came to the window.

"Can I borrow a half cup of sugar?" I asked.

She took the cup and disappeared, returning in a few minutes with it almost full. "Y'all got any bread?" she asked. "I need one more piece to make a sandwich."

"Maude wants to borrow a piece of bread," I told Mother.

"Give her two slices," Mother said.

I gave Maude two pieces of whole wheat.

"Elizabeth's coming back home today with her kids and Robert," she said. "Their furniture got put out in the street."

Elizabeth was her oldest sister and Robert her husband. He used to be a tailor but wasn't working now.

"Y'all gonna be crowded," I said.

"Yep," she answered, her head disappearing from the window.

I returned to the kitchen and told Mother Elizabeth was coming home.

"Lord, where they all gonna sleep?" she asked.

Maude and her sister, Rebecca, sixteen, had one bedroom, their mother the other, and their brother, Vallie, slept in the front room.

I sat down at the table and began to sip my tea, looking at the greasy walls lumpy with layers of paint over cracked plaster. Vomit-green, that's what Daddy called its color. The ceiling was dotted with brown and yellow water stains. Daddy had patched up the big leaks but it didn't do much good and when it rained outside it rained inside, too. The last time the landlord had been there to collect the rent Daddy told him the roof needed fixing and that if the ceiling fell down and hurt one of his kids he was going to pitch the landlord headfirst down the stairs. The landlord left in a hurry but that didn't get our leaks fixed.

The outside door slammed and my brother Sterling came into the kitchen and slumped down at the table. He was fourteen, brown-skinned, and lanky, his long, tight face always bunched into a frown, and today was no exception.

"Where's James Junior?" Mother asked.

"I'm not his keeper," Sterling grumbled. "I didn't see him at recess."

James Junior, my oldest brother, was a year older than Sterling, and good looking like Daddy. He was nicer than Sterling, too, but slow in his studies, always getting left back, and Sterling had already passed him in school and was going to graduate this month.

The door slammed shut again and I could tell from the heavy footsteps that it was Daddy. I jumped up and ran into the dining room hurling myself against him. He laughed and scooped me up in his arms, swinging me off the floor. Mother was always telling me that men were handsome, not beautiful, but she just didn't understand. Handsome meant one thing and beautiful something else and I knew for sure what Daddy was. Beautiful. In the first place he was a giant of a man, wide and thick and hard. He was dark brown, black really, with thick crinkly hair and a wide laughing beautiful mouth. I loved Daddy's mouth.

He sat down at the dining-room table and began pulling number slips from his pocket.

"Get the envelope for me, sugar."

I removed the drawer and handed him the envelope, smiling. "I dreamed a big catfish jumped off the plate and bit me, Daddy. The dream book gives five fourteen for fish. And Mrs. Mackey dreamed it was raining fish."

"Great God and Jim," Daddy cried, and we grinned at each other. "My chart gives a five to lead today. I'm gonna play a dollar on five fourteen straight and sixty cents combination."

Daddy said that of all the family my dreams hit the most. If 514 came out today we'd be rich, which would be a good thing 'cause Mother was always grumbling that we were playing all of our commission back on the numbers.

From force of habit I huddled close to the radiator, which was cold now. The green and red checkerboard linoleum around it was worn so thin you couldn't even see its pattern and there was a jagged hole in the floor near the pipe almost big enough to get your foot through. Daddy was always nailing cardboard and linoleum over that hole but it kept wearing out.

"Henrietta," Daddy called, "where are the boys?"

Mother came to the kitchen door. "Sterling's here eating, but James Junior ain't come home yet."

Daddy's fist hit the table with a suddenness which made me jump. "If that boy's stayed out of school again it's gonna be me and his behind. Sterling," he shouted, "where's your brother?"

"I ain't seen him since this morning," Sterling answered from the kitchen.

Daddy turned on Mother. "If that boy gets into any trouble I'm gonna let his butt rot in jail, you hear? I'm warning you. I've done told him time and time again to stop hanging out with those Ebony Earls, but his head is damned hard. All of them's gonna end up in Sing Sing, you mark my words, and ain't no Coffin ever been to jail before. Do you know that?"

Mother nodded. She also knew, as I did, that Daddy

would be the first one downtown to see about Junior if anything happened to him.

Junior had started hanging around with the Ebony Earls a few months ago, together with his buddies Sonny and Maude's brother Vallejo. Sterling didn't belong to the gang. He said gangs were stupid and boys who hung out together like that were morons.

Daddy started adding up the amounts of his number slips and counting the money. Mother sat down at the table beside him and said nervously that she heard Slim Jim had been arrested. He was a number runner like Daddy.

"Slim Jim is a fool," Daddy said. "His banker thinks he can operate outside the syndicate but nobody can buck Dutch Schultz. The cops will arrest anybody his boys finger, and they did just that. Fingered Slim Jim and his banker."

"Maybe you'd better stop collecting numbers now before . . ." Mother began nervously, but Daddy cut her off.

"For christsakes, Henrietta, let's not go through that again. How many times I gotta tell you it ain't much more dangerous collecting numbers than playing them. As long as the cops are paid off, which they are, they ain't gonna bother me. Schultz even pays off that stupid ass, Dodge, we've got for a district attorney, so stop worrying."

Mother played the numbers like everyone else in Harlem but she was scared about Daddy being a number runner. Daddy started working for Jocko on commission about six months ago when he lost his house-painting job, which hadn't been none too steady to begin with.

Jocko's name was really Jacques and he was a tall Creole from Haiti. He wore a blue beret cocked on the side of his head and had curly black hair and olive skin. Now, Jocko was handsome but he wasn't beautiful. He ran a candy store on Fifth Avenue and 117th Street as a front and everybody said he was real close to Big Boy Donatelli, his banker, who was real close to Dutch Schultz. Daddy said Jocko was as big a man in the syndicate as a colored man could get since the gangsters took over the numbers. Daddy said the gangsters controlled everything in Harlem—the numbers, the whores, and the pimps who brought them their white trade.

Mother grumbled: "I thought Mayor La Guardia say he was gonna clean up all this mess."

"If they really wanted to clean up this town," Daddy said, "they would stop picking on the poor niggers trying to hit a number for a dime so they won't starve to death. Where else a colored man gonna get six hundred dollars for one? What they need to do is snatch the gangsters banking the numbers, they're the ones raking in the big money. But the cops ain't about to cut off their gravy train. But you stop worrying now, Henrietta. Ain't nothing gonna happen to me, you hear?"

Mother nodded slowly. Then she looked at me. "Francie, get up from there and go on back to school before you be late again. Sterling," she yelled.

"Okay," he answered from the kitchen. "I'm comin'."

"Francie! Don't let me have to tell you again."

"Okay, Mother. I'm goin'. 'Bye, Daddy."

" 'Bye, sugar."

When I got downstairs I peaked outside but Sukie was nowhere in sight. I ran most of the way back to school but was good and late anyhow.

TWO

MRS. Oliver, my homeroom teacher, didn't even bawl me out for being late as I slid into my seat. I was disappointed. Maybe she didn't like me anymore.

I was in first-year junior high at P.S. 81 between St. Nicholas and Eighth Avenues, one of the worse girls' schools in Harlem, second only to P.S. 136 uptown. A brand-new baby was found flushed down the toilet at P.S. 136 last week. Nothing like that had happened at my school, at least not yet, but everything else did.

Everybody was excited at school today. There was a rumor that Saralee and Luisa's gang was gonna beat up all the teachers who were failing them. That would be just about every teacher in school except Mrs. Roberts. I don't think even Saralee, leader of the Ebonettes, would dare tangle with Mrs. Roberts. She taught us art and was the only colored teacher at our school and nobody messed with her. We didn't even take our magazines into her room, she was that tough.

The Ebonettes were the sister gang to the Ebony Earls, the roughest street fighters this side of Mt. Morris Park.

When the Earls warred with their rivals, the Harlem Raiders from uptown, blood flowed all up and down the avenue. When they weren't fighting each other, the gangs jumped the Jew boys who attended the synagogue on 116th Street or mugged any white man caught alone in Harlem after the sun went down. It got so bad that the insurance man from Metropolitan had to hire one of the Ebony Earls to ride around with him for protection when he made his collections. Yeah, the Earls were tough all right and the Ebonettes tried to be just as bad.

The bell rang and we all trooped down the hall to our first course. Maude was in my class and we walked together.

"I sure hope Saralee and them don't beat up Mrs. Oliver," she said. Maude had a square dark face and thick hair. If it wasn't for her bowlegs, which made her walk pigeon-toed, she wouldn't have been bad looking at all.

"I hope they don't," I agreed. I liked Mrs. Oliver. She was white-haired and looked like somebody's grandmother.

Maude and I sat together in Miss Haggerty's class. She was our arithmetic teacher and real pitiful, a pale stick of a woman, scared peeless most of the time. Now she mumbled that we would begin our lessons on page fifty-eight and to please take out our arithmetic books. Almost everybody, including me, took out our love stories and true confessions instead. We didn't even try to hide our magazines in Miss Haggerty's class and she was so terrified she just ignored them.

It was a good time for me to catch up on my love stories because Daddy wouldn't even let me bring those magazines inside the house. He said he didn't want to catch me reading such trash.

I usually paid attention to Miss Haggerty for the first five minutes, though, until I understood and could solve the problem. So today, when she asked for a volunteer for the blackboard, I raised my hand and stood up.

"Sit down," Saralee growled at me. I sat.

Miss Haggerty ignored us both. "Do we have a volunteer?" she asked again. Nobody moved.

"Well, then," Miss Haggerty said, walking to the blackboard and picking up a piece of chalk, "I'll work it out for you. Now the main thing to remember is—"

"Talk a little softer," Luisa said. "I can't concentrate on my story." The class tittered and Miss Haggerty's voice dropped to a whisper.

I sighed and turned my attention to my magazine. This was one problem I wasn't going to get because I sure wasn't going to tangle with Saralee and Luisa.

Luisa was Puerto Rican—white Puerto Rican—and was real pretty with her hair cut in a bob with bangs just like Claudette Colbert. Her running buddy, Saralee, was a burnt-brown color, with red hair, of all things. She was extra ugly. There was a rumor that Saralee was a bull-dagger. I don't know if that was true or not but she was certainly rough enough to be a man.

Both of them were older than the rest of us because they got left back so often, and everybody, including the teachers, were scared of them. They fought with razors and the Ebony Earls would beat up anybody that messed with their sister gang.

Instead of going back to our second class today, we were sent back to our homeroom and dismissed early. Before Saralee could round up her gang, the teachers they were gonna beat up were long gone.

I was glad, too, that we got out early. Now I could sneak home and avoid Sukie. She still went to the elementary school on Madison Avenue 'cause she had been left back twice.

Maude insisted on going down 118th Street on our way home and wouldn't you know Daddy would catch us? We was always sneaking around there hoping to see the prostitutes do something exciting. But they never did nothin' but sit with their dresses halfway up to their navels calling out at the men as they passed by, so we would walk along seeing whose dress was up the highest and if you could really see their thing 'cause they didn't wear no bloomers. And Daddy was always chasing us out of 118th Street and there he was now standing on China Doll's stoop waiting for us.

"How many times I got to tell you girls to stay out of this street?" he asked, looking very mad. "And you, Maude, I thought I could trust you."

"It wasn't my fault, Mr. Coffin, Francie wanted to—"

I kicked her ankle as Daddy cut her off.

"Your father told me before he died to make you mind. Both of you got a lickin' coming if I catch you in this block again, understand?"

"Yes, Daddy."

"Yes, Mr. Coffin."

We ran toward Fifth Avenue and turned the corner.

"What you tryin' to do," I asked Maude, "get me a whippin'?"

"You know your daddy ain't gonna whip you, Francie."

"Well, don't push my luck." I left her at my stoop and went on upstairs. That white man was still up there on the roof but I wasn't going up there by myself. If me and Sukie were still best friends I'd tell her about him and she'd know what to do to make us some safe money.

I ignored him when he whispered to me to come on up. I leaned against our door, the lock gave, and I went inside.

AFTER stringing some beans for dinner, I sat on the fire escape watching Sukie downstairs jumping rope with Maude and the Twins and some other kids from around the corner. The Twins looked so much alike we couldn't tell Maybelle from Florabelle so we just called them both the Twins.

They were playing Chase, skipping over the rope once and following the leader. I chanted with them: "Chase the white horse over the rocky mountain." I loved to jump rope and hated to be stuck up here on the fire escape instead of downstairs playing with them. My only consolation was that Sukie beat up on the others, too, when she wasn't picking on me.

That Sukie. I wondered what made her so mean? She was too pretty to be so evil, the color of a ripe peach where the yellow and the red meet, and her red-brown hair hung to her shoulders in two thick braids. I envied her that pretty, long hair. Where I was flat-chested and hollow, Sukie was plump and getting plumper. But she didn't like anybody, not even her mother and father. It was true that Papa Dan did wallow in King Kong all day long until he fell out from the stuff. But he was a nice, runty little man with bandy legs, always staggering around grinning like a fool and tipping his cap at every woman who passed by. He even grinned that time he bowed too low to Annette, a whore, and fell down the cellar steps. Everybody laughed but Sukie, who got so mad she called him a drunken sonafabitch when he crawled back up the stairs still smiling.

Sukie cursed all the time, and I had to strain some to keep up with her. Daddy didn't even want me to say darn.

He was always telling me: "It's darn today, damn tomorrow, and next week it'll be goddamn. You're going to
grow up to be a lady, Francie, and ladies don't curse."

I had to curse some though to stay friends with Sukie, but
I didn't play the dozens, that mother stuff, and I was scared
to take the Lord's name in vain.

Sukie's mother was always going up side her head 'cause
she was so sassy and telling her she was gonna be just like
her sister, China Doll. Mrs. Maceo was a tall thin woman,
dried up like a prune, but moriney like Sukie. She was always complaining that her drunken husband and hardheaded children were more of a cross than she could bear.
It was true that Sukie was hardheaded and China Doll was
a whore right around the corner. They called her China
Doll because she used to be so tiny and pretty with her
straight black hair and slanty eyes. She was getting pretty
plump lately, but the name still stuck.

Sukie said her mother loved her sister better than her, but
I don't know how she could say that when Mrs. Maceo
wouldn't even speak to China Doll.

It was on account of China that Sukie beat me up the last
time. All I asked her was why her sister hustled so close to
home and Sukie hauled off and punched me right in the
nose. I got away from her fast, and it was three weeks later
before she finally cornered me outside the candy store. You
wouldn't think anyone could stay so mad for three weeks
that they would bloody your nose, pull out a handful of
hair, loosen one tooth, and give you a solid kick in the side,
but Sukie did.

That same day we made up, I had to speak first, since
Sukie never would, and she told me just how China did it,
and we sneaked around the corner and watched her hustling

men in off the street. That Sukie. You never could tell what would set her off.

This time I hadn't said a mumbling word to her. She got mad at me on sight one day last week and asked if I was ready to fight. Naturally I wasn't ready. That Sukie. I wonder what made her so mean? What I ought to do is go on downstairs and get my whipping over with so we could be best friends again.

I looked over the railing. They were still jumping rope. "Chase the white horse over the rocky mountain."

It was after eleven o'clock and we were getting ready for bed. Sterling was in his room behind the kitchen and Daddy was in, too, but James Junior hadn't been home all day. I was helping Mother pull the couch I slept on in the front room away from the wall. Mother thought if the couch was in the middle of the floor the bedbugs wouldn't get me. But she thought wrong. Every Saturday Mother scalded the bedsprings with boiling water and Flit, which must have been those bugs' favorite recipe 'cause every night they marched right down that wall and bit me just the same.

When we were all settled down, Mother and Daddy started arguing in their bedroom next to me. She was asking Daddy one more time if she could go up in the Bronx and get some day's work.

"Why don't you stop nagging me, woman," Daddy said. "You know I don't want you doing housework."

"It's not what we want anymore," Mother said. "It's what we need. The children need shoes and school clothes. We're all in rags."

"They also need you to be home when they get out from school. Ain't I having enough troubles now, for christsakes? What you want to start that shit all over again for? We ain't starving yet."

"We ain't far from it."

Daddy didn't answer.

After a slight pause Mother said: "Adam."

"What?"

"The relief people are giving out canned beef and butter. Mrs. Taylor got on last week. I don't know when's the last time we've had any butter."

"And we may never have any again if I've got to let those damned social workers inside my house to get it. Bastards act like it's their money they're handing out. We ain't going on relief, Henrietta, and don't ask me again."

"So what we gonna do? If you could find some work . . ."

"They ain't got jobs for the ofays so how in hell you expect me to find anything?" There was a pause and when Daddy spoke again his voice was gentle. "I'm gonna play the piano at three rent parties next weekend. I oughta make ten dollars at each one. That will help some. It's gonna be all right, baby, so you stop worrying now, and trust me. You hear?"

Mother didn't answer. I trusted Daddy. I wondered how come she didn't.

A few minutes later I heard the dining-room door squeak open. Damn that squeak. If James Junior was gonna try and sneak home in the middle of the night, why didn't he oil that noisy door? Daddy heard him, too, jumped out of bed, and ran into the dining room hollering at the top of his voice: "Where you been all day, James Junior?" And before Junior could answer him Daddy yelled: "Don't you hear me talking to you? Answer me before I knock you back down those steps."

Me and Mother crept into the dining room, and Sterling, scowling fiercely, came down the hall from the kitchen.

"I been over on Madison Avenue with Sonny and Vallie," James Junior said. He was big for fifteen and good looking just like Daddy.

"You been down in that cellar with that gang?"

"It's a club room," Junior said.

"It's a den of thieves," Daddy roared. "You cut school today, too?"

Junior didn't answer. He wasn't defiant like Sterling would have been, but he wasn't scared either.

"Get me my strop, Francie."

"Don't beat him, Daddy."

"Get me my strop."

Trembling, I went into the bathroom and pulled the discolored razor strop down from its rusty nail and took it to Daddy. If only Junior would promise to stop playing hooky and hanging out with the Ebony Earls, I knew Daddy wouldn't beat him.

But Junior was stubborn and as Daddy raised the blackened piece of leather over his head, Junior didn't say a word. Daddy swung the strop with all his might and the thick end lashed into Junior's shoulders. He winced, but didn't cry out.

"I'm warning you for the last time," Daddy said, breathing hard, "you ain't gonna disgrace this family. Stay away from that damned gang, you hear?" The strop snapped across Junior's chest. "Play hooky one more time and I'm gonna kill you." Another blow landed on Junior's back. "You want to be like Skeeter Madison? Dead in some alley because of some senseless gang fight?"

Junior dodged the next blow, knocking over a chair.

ocococococococ DADDY WAS A NUMBER RUNNER

"Or maybe you want to join your friend Pee Wee in Sing Sing? You hear me talking to you?"

"Answer him," I begged silently, but Junior didn't open his mouth. He leaped over a chair and Daddy hemmed him up in a corner. The strop rose and fell harder and harder. Junior tucked his head under his hunched shoulders as the blows rained down on his back.

Suddenly I was crying and then screaming.

I heard Mother's voice rise sharply over my screams: "Stop it, James Adam. That's enough."

Daddy stopped, looking around confused. Then he dropped the strop and strode into the bedroom, slamming the door.

"Francie, stop that screaming," Mother said. "Anybody would think you were being murdered."

She turned to Junior and her voice softened. "You know better than to make your father mad like that, James Junior. One of these days he's gonna kill you. All of you go on to bed now."

I went back to my couch and dried my eyes on the sheet. Daddy had whipped poor Junior with the thick end of the strop. Whether you got whipped with the thick or thin end depended on how bad you had been. I'd never been whipped with the thick end yet, in fact, Daddy never whipped me, not because I was all that good but because I was his favorite.

Why hadn't Junior just promised to stop messing around with that stupid gang? He wasn't mean enough to be an Ebony Earl nohow. How could he ever mug anybody, good-natured and nice as he was. Why, when he smiled his whole face laughed. He wasn't like old Sterling who didn't like anybody and whose narrow, old man's face was full of dark, secret shadows.

co 32 co

Still, Junior wouldn't get whipped so much if he spent his time reading and studying like Sterling who was always stinking up the house with his nasty chemicals. You would think Junior would feel bad 'cause his baby brother was gonna graduate before he did, but he didn't seem to care at all.

On the weekends Daddy gave Sterling a few dimes and he'd go down to Forty-second Street and do real good shining shoes on a stand he made from an orange crate. Daddy said he wished Junior was that enterprising, but Junior acted like he didn't hear him. Anyway, he never did make himself a shoeshine box and I don't think he knew the way to Forty-second Street.

After the house quieted down I sneaked past my parents' bedroom and tiptoed to the back.

My brothers' room behind the kitchen was so small that the cot and dresser took up all the floor space. Junior slept at the top of the bed and Sterling at the bottom.

"You all right, Junior?" I sat on the edge of the bed and he scooted over.

"Yeah, Francie. I'm all right. But I'm too big for Daddy to beat like that anymore. That's the last whippin' I'm gonna take."

I touched a welt on his face and he winced. Two dark lines ran down his cheeks. They were tears.

"He beat *me* like that," Sterling grumbled from the foot of the bed, "and I'm gonna take that strop away from him and use it on his head."

"You and who else?" I asked. "You can't whip Daddy." But Sterling just might try it and then Daddy would kill him for sure. I turned back to Junior. "Why didn't you just promise Daddy to stop hanging out with the Ebony Earls? That's all he wanted."

" 'Cause I ain't gonna stop, that's why." He wiped his face with the back of his hand and lit a cigarette butt.

"The Ebony Earls had an initiation meeting tonight," Sterling said. "That's where you been so late, Junior? Getting initiated?"

"Yeah," Junior answered. "That's where I been. I'm a full-fledged member of the war council now."

"But why, Junior?" I asked, feeling sick. "Why?"

"Man, nobody messes with an Ebony Earl," Junior said slowly, thinking it out. "People see me walking down the street, they say, there goes James Adam Coffin, Junior. He's a bad stud. Everybody respects a bad stud. Don't make no difference whether you're bad or not, just as long as people think you are. And you naturally get a rep just by belonging to the Ebony Earls. You automatically become somebody."

"Bullshit," Sterling said.

"You come with me to the next meeting, Sterling," Junior said. "You ain't gonna get nowhere with that shoeshine box, man. What kind of money is that? Next meeting you come with me."

"Don't go with him, Sterling," I cried. "Stay away from that stupid gang. You always said yourself they was stupid."

"Shut up," Sterling said, "and mind your own business. Who invited you in here anyhow? Go on back to bed."

"I can't. I'm scared to go through the kitchen. I hear a rat."

"You wasn't scared to come in here with your nosy self."

I started to whimper, and with a curse Sterling got up and walked me back to Mother's bedroom door.

"Sterling, you ain't gonna join the gang, too. Please don't."

He shoved me through the door roughly, but when he spoke his voice was gentle. "Don't worry none about me,

Francie. I can take care of myself, you hear?" He touched my face awkwardly and then he was gone.

As I made my way back to the couch, I thought, that was the first time in a long time Sterling had spoken nice to me.

THREE

SUKIE finally cornered me one afternoon. I had taken my usual place on the fire escape and was reading a book of fairy tales from the library—although I knew I was too old for fairy tales—when Mother called me and told me to go uptown and borrow three dollars from Aunt Hazel. She handed me a nickel for carfare.

"What if she ain't home?" I asked. Aunt Hazel lived on 131st Street.

"Then walk back. You've walked that far before."

I sneaked on the subway to save the nickel and then walked down Lenox Avenue to 131st Street.

Aunt Hazel's hallway smelled like all the other hallways in Harlem. Funky. I walked up one flight and knocked on her door.

"Who is it?"

"It's me, Aunt Hazel. Francie."

I heard her slide the chain lock off and then the door opened and Aunt Hazel was hugging me and pulling me inside. She smelled nice, like cake baking.

The light was on in her living room, which was always

dark, 'cause no sun could squeeze through that narrow window which was smack up against the wall of the house next door. That's why we lived on the top floor, Daddy said, so we could snatch a little sunshine. Aunt Hazel's rooms were tiny but spotless, with everything in its place, not junky like ours, and I loved to come here.

"Look who's come to visit," Aunt Hazel said, as I followed her into the living room.

Mr. Mulberry was seated at a card table where he and Aunt Hazel had been playing cooncan and drinking gin. He jumped up and hugged me and made me sit in his chair.

Mr. Mulberry was a very tall, very black West Indian who worked as handyman for the same family Aunt Hazel worked for. She slept in and so did he and was off on Thursdays, same as her. I don't know where Mr. Mulberry lived, but whenever I came to visit Aunt Hazel he was here. Sometimes Mr. and Mrs. Atwater, who also slept in, were also here, and the four of them would be playing whist, drink or smell, laughing and banging the cards down on the table with a flourish. The winners would get a drink, and the losers would have to wait until they won a hand before they got a sip.

"Get the child something to eat, Hazel," Mr. Mulberry said, "and I'll run downstairs and buy her a soda."

"Thank you, Mr. Mulberry," I said politely, "but please don't go to all of that trouble," hoping of course that he would ignore me, which he did.

"It's my pleasure, Francie," he said in his nice West Indian accent, and left.

Aunt Hazel commented as usual on how skinny I was as she pattered about in the kitchen fixing me a fried-fish sandwich and a glass of milk. I wasn't very fond of fish, but I ate it anyway and it was good. Then she gave me a piece of pound cake and Mr. Mulberry was back with a cherry soda. They both watched me eat as if I couldn't digest the food without their help.

"Another piece of cake, darling?"

"Yes, thank you, Aunt Hazel."

While I was eating the second piece I told her Mother wanted to borrow three dollars. I had made this trip many times before—a one-way trip 'cause though I often was sent uptown to borrow money I was never sent to pay it back.

"You sure three dollars is enough?" Aunt Hazel asked, as she handed me three crumpled bills.

I smiled at her. Good old Aunt Hazel. She never turned us down.

Aunt Hazel was what Daddy called a big beautiful girl. She was no girl, though, older than Mother, and I don't know about that beautiful part either. Daddy was always saying somebody was beautiful—some black girl with thick lips and a wide nose who everybody else thought was downright homely. Me and Mother would look at each other and shake our heads sadly when Daddy went into his black beauty bit.

"You're blind in one eye," Mother would tell him, "and deaf in the other."

Not that Aunt Hazel was ugly. In fact, she looked like Mother, only better looking, with long hair she wore in a bun on top of her head. She still had all her teeth and she laughed a lot. She was jollier than Mother, too, which probably came from drinking gin and wine. Mother didn't drink a thing.

Aunt Hazel didn't have any children, and was always saying she had no family in this world but us. She had been married once but the louse ran off and left her before I was born.

I squeezed the last drop of soda from my glass, got up, and was swallowed in Aunt Hazel's arms again. I said good-bye to Mr. Mulberry and left.

I walked back home through Mt. Morris Park. When I was two blocks away I looked down Fifth Avenue and it seemed as if a huge crowd was gathered right in front of my house. My heart started its crazy thumping and I slowed down to a crawl.

This had happened to me before, especially at twilight. My vision became blurred and I couldn't tell the difference between a normal overflowing street and a crowd of people. Crowds always meant something terrible—a fight or a killing or somebody had fallen off the roof or been run over by a car. So anytime I saw a crowd I was scared that something awful had happened to my brothers.

I crept closer. It was a crowd all right, right in front of my stoop. I saw Maude Caldwell at the edge of the crowd, staring at something on the ground. I inched toward her, my eyes glued to her face. If her face crumpled with horror when she saw me, if she raced forward to be the first to tell me the bad news, then I would know that something terrible had happened to Junior or Sterling.

When I was next to her I whispered, "Maude."

She looked at me and nodded and then turned away. I fell apart with relief. Her look had been normal.

"What's happening?" I asked.

Before she could answer a woman screamed. I pushed through the crowd in time to see China Doll get knocked off her feet and bounce on her plump behind as she hit the pavement. A strange brown man snatched her up and knocked her down again with a swinging blow to her head.

"Do it to your mother, you cocksucker," China screamed.

The man socked her again.

"It's her new pimp," Maude explained, adding unnecessarily, "He's beating the shit out of her."

Nobody in the crowd made a move to help China. You just didn't interfere in Harlem street fights, especially between a man and his woman. She might jump up and whip whoever came to her rescue.

I hated to see China Doll get knocked down like that though. She was still little, but plump, and so pretty with her slanty eyes and straight black hair.

She called the man a string of motherfuckers but he had turned away, shut of the matter. Finally, she got to her feet.

"What are you looking at, you black bastards," she yelled at the crowd. A path opened before her and she limped to the corner and turned down 118th Street.

It was then that Sukie saw me. Naturally I felt sorry for Sukie, seeing her sister get beat up like that, and I was going to tell her so when I remembered that she was mad at me. It was her face which made me remember. She was moving toward me, her face red with rage, her lips drawn back over her teeth in a snarl.

I didn't even feel it when she socked me. I just hit the pavement, but *my* behind didn't bounce. I fell on my tailbone and it hurt.

The crowd, which had begun to drift, came back for the new fight. Someone above me chuckled: "These Maceo girls are a fighting mess." I couldn't help but agree.

Sukie's whole body landed flat on top of me, pinning my legs to the ground. I tried to rock her off but she was too heavy. She grabbed a handful of hair and yanked, setting my scalp on fire.

I squeezed Mother's three dollars in my fist and swung at Sukie with both arms. My weak blows didn't bother her at all. She kept punching me in the face. My nose spurted blood and I began to cry softly. My thrashing became wilder as I tried to overturn her. She had her knees in my chest now. A hard blow landed on my Adam's apple and I started to choke.

Someone mercifully pulled Sukie off me. For a moment I didn't even know the fight was over. My jaw was throbbing and I knew another tooth was loose. I dragged my hand under my nose and looked at the smear of blood on it as I tried to swallow my sobs. Avoiding all eyes, I got up, and this time a path opened up for me. I ran home.

Inside the hallway I really started to bawl: "Mother. Mother." By the time I reached the fifth floor, Mother was standing at the top of the stairs.

"Sukie beat me up and I didn't do nothing."

Mother pulled me into the bathroom and made me hold my head back until my nose stopped bleeding. She gently washed my face and poked about the bruises, putting iodine on my scratches.

"Sukie's been waiting to beat me up for two weeks."

"Was Aunt Hazel home?"

"Yes. Sukie's always picking on me." I handed Mother the three dollars. "I walked home and saved the nickel. Can I have it?" I didn't mention that I had also sneaked on the subway and saved that nickel, too.

"I was going to give you a nickel anyhow," Mother said. "You didn't have to walk back home."

"I didn't do nothing to Sukie, Mother. She's always picking on me."

"You been running away from her for two weeks," Mother said, "but you still had to fight her, didn't you?"

"Yeah, but . . ."

"And in those two weeks every day you got more scared of her."

"She's bigger than me."

"Francie, you can beat anything, anybody, if you face up to it and if you're not scared."

"But, Mother, Daddy said ladies don't fight with their fists in the street like common tramps. That's what he said."

"There are more ways to fight, Francie, than with your fists."

"I wish somebody would tell Sukie that."

I spoke first to Sukie the next day and we were best friends again. She had stolen a quarter from her mother's purse that morning and wanted to know what I had.

"Nothing," I muttered, ashamed to admit I was too scared to steal my mother's change. It wasn't exactly that I was scared. I had taken a dime from Mother's pocketbook once, and she had spent a half hour on her knees looking for it under the couch and worrying about that lousy dime all day. I could never bring myself to pinch anything from her again.

Sukie bought two caramel lollipops and gave me one. When we were best friends she was very generous, buying me whatever she got for herself. Maybe I could get a nickel from Daddy and tomorrow I would tell her I picked his pocket. That oughta make her happy.

"GET ten cents' worth of ground meat and ask the butcher for a soup bone."

"Yes, Mother."

I had just come home from school, and I ran back downstairs and into the meat store on the corner. It was empty except for Mr. Morristein, the plump butcher whose hair was so nappy it looked colored.

"I want ten cents' worth of hamburger meat and my mother says to please give her a soup bone."

"Come to the end of the counter, Francie, and let me see how big you are growing."

I sighed and scuffed up the sawdust on the floor as I walked to the end of the display case holding the meat. Mr. Morristein, in his scroungy white smock, patted my shoulder and his hand slipped down and squeezed my breast.

"My, my. Such a nice big girl you are getting."

His voice had gone funny again as if his tongue was too thick for his mouth. I stood there patiently while his hands fumbled over my body. Anytime I came to the butcher and no one else was there I had to stand still for this nonsense.

"Mr. Morristein. My mother is in a hurry."

His hands were now rubbing my thigh and my dress was halfway up. The bell over the door rang and Mr. Morristein scuttled back around the end of the counter as Mrs. Mackey entered, beaming her happy smile at me.

"How are you, Francie?"

"Fine, Mrs. Mackey."

"The second figure out yet?"

"No, ma'am. Just the two in the lead."

"I sure hope it's two oh two. I dreamed about my dead husband last night and that play's for his name. Tell your father I want him to play the piano at my whist party next week. He's all booked up for this weekend, ain't he?"

"I think so, Mrs. Mackey."

"Here's your meat, Francie. And two soup bones I am sending to your mother."

"Thank you, Mr. Morristein."

Two soup bones. I hoped Mother would be impressed. I passed the bakery shop and Max the Baker was outside sweeping the tile. I got extra rolls from him, too, whenever he got the chance to feel me. Max the Baker was very sorry looking. Everything about him from his pinpoint head to his narrow feet was tiny, and he was pasty white not dark like the other Jews on the block. His gray tomcat came out of the bakery and rubbed against his leg. I stuck my tongue out at Max the Baker and raced into my hallway.

Sukie hollered after me. "You comin' back down? Let's go to the park."

"I'll ask my mother."

I ran upstairs and pushed against our door and the lock sprang open.

"Mr. Morristein gave us two soup bones," I told Mother. "Can I go to the park with Sukie?"

"Two soup bones. That's the second time this week he's given us something extra. What's got into that old Jew? You can go to the park but I want you back up here before six so you can set the table. You hear?"

"Yes, Mother."

It was a lovely day, warm, but not too hot. At Mt. Morris Park we climbed to the bell tower and watched the kids below playing in the playground. I liked to swing on the swings, sailing up high over the treetops. If you closed your eyes to slits and peered through the green lace the leaves made, you could imagine you were someplace else. Any-place you wanted to be. But Sukie didn't want to go swing-ing so we came up here where the bums were sprawled on the benches and stretched out on the grass.

Sukie left the path and clambered through the under-brush and I followed her. We came upon a little clearing completely surrounded by shrubbery so that it made a little cave. An old white man was sitting on the ground watching us intently. His chin was gray with stubble and the rest of his face was splotchy and red. His khakis were so dirty they were stiff. We stopped a few feet away from him.

"You girls wanna make a nickel?" He started to rise.

"Stay where you are," Sukie commanded.

"Aw, come on," the man pleaded, falling back onto the grass. "I won't hurt you. I just wanna feel you a little."

"No feeling," Sukie said.

"Just a look then," the man said desperately as Sukie turned away. "Just pull down your pants and let me look."

"A nickel apiece?" Sukie asked.

"A nickel apiece."

The man flipped a coin at each of us and we caught it before it hit the ground, being careful to keep our distance. Sukie lifted up her skirt and pulled down her bloomers and I did the same, watching the man's face all the time. His gray stubble turned purple and his tongue darted in and out between his lips like a puppy lapping up milk.

"Come closer." He started to crawl toward us. We pulled up our bloomers and, turning, darted through the hedge. Crossing over the path, we kept on running down the hill, laughing and shrieking as we lost our footing and rolled to the bottom. Giggling, we got to our feet and brushed the grass off our clothes.

I was glad Sukie never let any of these bums touch us. It was bad enough having the butcher and Max the Baker always sneaking a feel, but at least they were clean. Then there was the men on the roof showing off their privates and the man in the movies with his fumbling hands—that little bald-headed man who had stopped hanging around my roof and now followed me to the show.

I had dropped my nickel in our flight down the hill, but Sukie still had hers. We walked slowly home and she bought us both a two-cents seltzer water from Mr. Rathbone. He was a fat little Jew who ran the candy store on our block, together with his wife and round-faced daughter, Rachel. They were nice and lived on 110th Street across from

Central Park. Rachel was in her twenties and was the prettiest Jewish girl I ever saw. At least Mr. Rathbone was never fumbling at me, neither was Mr. Lipschwitz, the plumber, who had given us his old furniture and the piano.

It was after six o'clock when I got home but Mother didn't notice I was late.

"Put the jumper in the box," she said, as I walked into the kitchen, "then set the table."

I really didn't like to jump that box, I was that afraid of electricity. Mother was putting dirty clothes into the double sink to soak. She was always either soaking clothes or scrubbing them or hanging them out on the line. With all of that activity we should have been super clean but somehow we weren't. Anyhow, it seemed like the least I could do was put the jumper in, so I dragged a chair under the meter box and climbed up on it. I took the metal wire from behind the box where we hid it, and opening the box, I inserted the two prongs behind the fuse the way Daddy had showed me. I got down from the chair, pulled the light chain, and the light came on.

Our electricity had been cut off for months for nonpayment, so Daddy had made the jumper and we used it in the evenings when it started to get dark. We didn't keep the jumper in all day because the electric man came around once a month to read the meter and we never knew when he was coming. He used a little gadget to get the meter box hot so he could read it, and by using the jumper, the meter didn't register.

Daddy said almost everybody in Harlem used a jumper and it was a shame there was no way to jump the gas. When our gas got turned off, we used Mrs. Maceo's or Mrs. Caldwell's stove. They used ours a few times, too, so it was all right, but everybody tried to keep the gas from being turned off and thanked God for the electric jumpers.

I started to set the table.

Junior and Sterling came home on time and everybody was in a good mood for a change. After dinner I helped Mother wash and dry the dishes real fast so the roaches wouldn't have a snack, then we all went into the front room to help Daddy practice for his weekend parties.

The piano Mr. Lipschwitz had given us was real old but Daddy kept it tuned, and though the ivory was off most of the keys, it had a nice, mellow tone. Daddy played by ear and could swing any piece after he heard it only once.

Junior was leaning against the piano singing a new song he had heard on the radio. Daddy picked out the melody the first time around, then put a rocking bass to it and had another song to add to his rep-or-tor, as he called it. Sterling wrote down the names of the songs as me and Junior sang them. Sterling couldn't sing a lick and neither could Mother, but me and Junior had fairly nice voices, sweet but on the weak side.

"Listen to that bass, dumpling," Daddy said to me, swinging into "Ain't Misbehavin'." "Sounds just like Old Fats, don't it?"

It tickled Daddy to sound like Fats Waller, who, according to Daddy, was boss man of the ivories. Then Daddy played the blues and began to sing:

Trouble in mind,
I'm blue,
But I won't be blue always.
The sun's gonna shine
In my back door someday.

Daddy's voice was coarse, straining at the high notes, but very spirited. We sang along with him, even Mother, with her no-nothing treble. Sterling had the good grace to hum, off key.

Cold empty bed
Pains in my head
Feel like ol' Ned
Wish I was dead
What did I do
To be so black and blue?

Then it was ten o'clock and Daddy left for his parties. I sat down at the piano and did a few riffs which sounded pitiful. I just didn't have Daddy's talents and that was plain. I had studied music off and on since I was eight—mostly off 'cause though Miss Jackson, my teacher up on 130th Street, only charged a quarter a lesson, Mother didn't often have that quarter. It didn't seem fair that I just couldn't sit down and play like Daddy did but had to go through all that jive of reading music and playing that Blue Danube thing. I picked out "Stormy Weather" with one hand, and then went to bed.

MOTHER said it was a catastrophe.

Daddy said it wasn't all that bad and for God's sake don't go getting hysterical.

What happened was that at the rent parties Daddy played for he had been offered more King Kong than money, and since he was not a drinking man he had accepted his tips in food. He had eaten hoppin' john and chitlins and fried chicken all weekend long, and had brought home only nine dollars and thirty cents from the three parties instead of the thirty dollars he had expected.

Mother was so mad she was trembling. "I can't sit around here and watch these children go hungry," she said. "Either you let me go up in the Bronx and find some day's work or we'll have to get on relief. There ain't no other way."

Mother kept at it until finally Daddy hollered that a man couldn't have any peace in his own home and yes, goddammit, go on up in the Bronx and find some work if she wanted to.

On Monday morning Mother took the subway to Grand Concourse. She told me later that she waited on the sidewalk under an awning with the other colored women. When a white lady drove up and asked how much she charged by the hour, Mother said thirty-five cents and was hired for three half days a week by a Mrs. Schwartz.

FOUR

I pushed open the Caldwells' door which was seldom locked. "Hey, Maude," I yelled, "you home?"

"You got to shout like that?" Robert asked, coming out of the bedroom. "Ain't nobody deaf around here. Maude's in the front room."

"I'm sorry, Robert." I walked past him. He sure was one evil black West Indian, and especially so since he lost his precious car. I know that nearly killed him, having to give that car up. When he used to visit Fifth Avenue with Elizabeth before they got dispossessed and had to move in with her mother, he would holler at us kids something awful just 'cause we touched his old shiny chrome.

"Y'all keep your greasy hands off my car," he would command, and pay one of the boys a nickel to see that we didn't touch it. He was evil all right, but good looking, with broad shoulders and thick arms and legs.

I went into the front room. Vallie, dressed in a polka-dot dress, was poking about the sofa, looking under the cushions. With his round baby face he looked almost like a girl except for the greasy stocking cap on his head.

"Hello, Vallie."

"Hi, Francie. Hey, Maude," he called. "You know where Ma hid my pants?"

"The last place you'd be expected to look for them," Maude said from the fire escape. "In the clothes closet."

Vallie went into the bedroom and came back with his pants. He slipped them under the dress which he then whipped off over his head. His mother came into the room. I loved Mrs. Caldwell, she was that jolly and nice and fat and warm with her West Indian accent.

"So, my son, you've found your pants, huh?"

"Yes, Ma."

"You going to come back upstairs tonight at a decent hour?"

"Yes, Ma."

Mrs. Caldwell sighed. "I don't know why your father upped and died like he did leaving me with all these problems."

"You making more problems, Ma, than you have to," Vallie said. "What you tryin' to do, make a sissy out of me or something, making me wear Rebecca's clothes?"

"Better a live sissy than a dead little boy," she said, going to Vallie and straightening his shirt collar. "Ain't that right, Francie?"

"I guess so, Mrs. Caldwell."

Vallie stayed out in the street so much that when he did come home his mother hid his pants and made him wear his sister's clothes knowing he wouldn't sneak downstairs dressed like a girl.

"When you come back upstairs," Mrs. Caldwell told Vallie, "bring me two penny licorice sticks."

"Okay," Vallie said, holding out his hand. His mother dropped two cents into it. She dearly loved licorice sticks.

"Francie's here," Mrs. Caldwell told Maude. "Come off of that fire escape and talk to her."

Maude grumbled something but didn't make a move, so when Sonny hollered down from the roof for Vallie to hurry on up there, I followed him. Sukie was there, too.

"Hey, man," Sonny said to Vallie. "What took you so long? I called you three times."

"I had to find my pants."

"Francie," Sonny said, looking at me from under his sleepy eyes, "you sure are getting tall for a girl and *skin-nay!*"

"Hello, Sonny." I couldn't think of anything else to say, as usual, so I turned to Sukie. "Hi. Where you been all day?"

"Playing jacks with you up till ten minutes ago. What's the matter, you losin' your mind or something?"

I could have killed her. She always did that, showed me up in front of the boys.

"Come on," Sonny said, running toward the back of the roof. "Let's jump over the alley." He stopped short at the end of the roof and bowed. "Ladies first."

I trailed behind them, deciding that no matter how bad they teased me I wasn't gonna jump. Everybody almost had jumped over that old alley at some time or another except me. Anytime I saw a crowd in the street looking down at something near the alley, I thought that James Junior or Sterling had finally missed and fell while jumping over it, and no amount of teasing could make me do it.

Vallie always teased the most. Now he was saying: "A long-legged gal like you ought to be able to stretch from one side of that alley to the other."

"Ain't it the truth," Sukie agreed, and showing off she backed up and with a flying leap jumped to the other roof.

Then just to show how easy it was, she jumped back to our side again.

"Go ahead, Francie," Vallie urged. "Sukie's legs ain't even as long as yours."

"Leave me alone, pretty brown girl," I said, knowing that would make him mad. Any hint about him wearing Rebecca's clothes did.

Vallie stopped smiling and leaped at me. In ducking away from him I bumped into Sonny who grabbed my arm.

"Should I throw her over the roof for you, Vallie?" he asked.

Sonny was big for his age and square as a box, and as he held me I thought for a moment that he might not be kidding. Vallie didn't answer.

"Throw her over," Sukie said calmly.

"Y'all stop playing like that with me," I said, nervous now. "I'm gonna tell Junior."

"You can't tell nobody nothing if you're dead, dead, dead," Sonny said, his eyes half-closed.

"Aw, leave her alone," Vallie said.

Sonny released me, crossed the divider to the next roof and ran to the door. "Y'all wait here a minute," he said, "I'll be right back." He disappeared inside and a moment later came back out holding a black cat by the nape of its neck. A rope dangled from its head and apparently Sonny had tied the cat to the banister earlier.

"Whatcha gonna do with your grandma's cat?" Sukie asked.

"Wait and see." Sonny walked to the side of the roof and dangled the cat over the edge. Suddenly his fingers sprung open and the cat fell.

I screamed.

"You sonofabitch," Vallie yelled. "Whatcha do that for?"

"Come on," Sonny said, running toward the door.

Vallie followed him and I trailed behind, not wanting to go. I turned around to see if Sukie was coming and saw that she was quietly vomiting up her lunch.

I raced down the stairs behind the boys to the basement and out into the yard where the cat lay in a tangled mess of broken bones and black fur slimy with blood.

Sonny bent over the cat and then straightened up. "The bastard is dead."

"What the hell did you expect?" Vallie asked. "For him to jump up and kiss you?"

"I expected him to have nine lives like they always say a cat has," Sonny said. He turned away in disgust. "They lied."

I started to whimper.

"It's all right, Francie," Vallie said, pulling me up the basement steps. "Sonny is just a crazy nigger. I hope his grandma whips his ass for killing her cat like that."

AFTER breakfast on Sunday Mother and I went to Abyssinian Baptist Church to hear Adam. Mother was a born Methodist but she had been going to Abyssinian ever since we lived in Brooklyn. The Old Man was preaching then, Adam's father, and I used to think that he looked just like God, with his long white hair and all.

We never could get Daddy to go to church with us, although he did admit that Adam had done a lot of good in Harlem, particularly last year when he opened a free food kitchen and fed a thousand people a week. Adam was also a leader in the rent strikes. Daddy said that was good, otherwise more people would have been set out on the street.

But on the whole, Daddy would have nothing to do with churches and preachers.

"King James of England wrote the Bible," he was always telling Mother, "and he made you niggers happy hewers of wood and told you to serve your masters faithfully and you'd get your reward in heaven. You all believe that shit and been worshiping a white Jesus ever since. How in the hell could God take the black earth and make himself a white man out of it? Answer me that?"

But Mother never tried to answer. She just hauled me off with her to church and sometimes sent me to Mt. Olivet Sunday school on 120th Street and Lenox Avenue. Daddy didn't care whether we went to Sunday school or not, so naturally James Junior and Sterling never went.

Church was packed this morning. It was a hot day and the sweat rolled down the congregation's faces as they joined the choir in singing:

What are they doing in heaven today?
Where sin and sorrow are all washed away,
Where peace abides like a river they say,
What are they doing there now?

That song always made me think of the dead, and I was wondering what Mr. Caldwell was doing in heaven today when the lady next to me started screaming:

"Praise his Holy name. Do, Jesus. Do."

I inched away from her so nobody would think we were together. She threw her fat self around like a top, and I felt like disappearing under the floorboards. Why did they have to shout and holler like that? Adam stood up to preach. He was a handsome, large man, so white he could have passed. Even before he opened his mouth, the lady next to me shouted again:

"Preach His Holy word, Adam. Thank Thee, Father, for Adam Powell, Jr." Still shouting, she threw her arms out wide, almost knocking me sideways, then stiffened and leaped up. A nurse in white came running and grabbed the woman's hands and eased her back into her seat. The nurse began fanning her and I turned to Mother. She smiled at me and I smiled back, moving closer to her.

First Adam talked about Haile Selassie asking the League of Nations for protection from Mussolini and how they was ignoring him. Then he almost wept about that terrible lynching in Florida I had read about in *The Amsterdam News*. His sermon was about Moses leading the Israelites out of Egypt and how the Negro today was in worse bondage and had to free himself.

I liked Adam. He talked about things that were happening today and preached such a powerful sermon that the sisters shouting "Hallelujah" and "Amen" kept me from dozing off. By the time he finished preaching they were swooning and jumping up and down all over the church. As I followed Mother out, I was glad that while she loved Adam dearly, she wasn't the shouting kind.

The next day after school I banged on Sukie's door and when she didn't answer I went looking for her in the street but she was nowhere to be found. I went up to her roof, which was two houses down from mine, and climbed down the fire escape to her apartment which was on the top floor, too. There she was looking out the window.

"Come on in, Francie."

"I knocked a little while back but you didn't answer," I said.

"I didn't hear you. I was lookin' out the window."

"What you wanna do today?" I asked. "If we had some money we could go to the show."

"I got fifteen cents," she said. "What you got?"

"Nothin'. But maybe I can get a dime from my father if I can find him."

"Okay, let's go." She didn't have to ask anybody if she could go to the show because there was nobody to ask. Papa Dan was drunk in some hallway somewhere, and Mrs. Maceo was a cook for a private family and didn't come home until around nine o'clock at night.

I found my father in Jocko's candy store. No, we don't have no homework, I told him, and he gave me a dime and me and Sukie walked on down to 116th Street.

We couldn't decide whether to go to the Jewel or Regun Theatre and was arguing about it. There was a cowboy picture I wanted to see at the Jewel with Ken Maynard, my favorite. Sukie wanted to see "Zombies from Haiti" at the Regun. I don't know why I wasted my time arguing with her 'cause we walked right past the Jewel and headed for the Regun farther down the street and I knew that picture was gonna scare me so much I wouldn't be able to sleep.

That white bald-headed man who used to try and get me to come up on the roof and now followed me to the show every chance he got was standing outside the Jewel. I stuck my tongue out at him as I passed. He only bothered me when I was alone so I knew he wasn't gonna follow us.

Right in front of the Regun six or seven people was laughing at a drunk, a roly-poly black man trying to walk straight. How he could stand up at all was a miracle. With every step he took he tilted so far sideways that everybody held their breath thinking he was gonna fall flat on his face, and when he made it without tumbling over, they whistled and hollered: "You did it, baby. Go, man, go!"

The man grinned at them, happy 'cause they was happy, took another staggering step and slammed into the pavement. There was an instant of silence, a fear that maybe he'd hurt himself, but when he hunched himself up on his knees, the people cheered. After trying to get to his feet twice, he finally thought better of it and began to crawl on his hands and knees. The people laughed and he giggled with them.

Then an ofay cop walked up. "Okay, break it up, let's get movin'," he ordered. He grabbed the drunk in the collar and hauled him to his feet. The fat man's legs caved in and he stumbled, almost pulling the cop down on top of him. The people laughed. The cop, red in the face, swung his billy up side the drunk's head. The fat man pulled away, dropping to his knees again, and rolled himself up in a ball, his head tucked under his arms. The cop kicked his behind and then brought his nightstick down on the man's shoulder.

I grunted, feeling the pain. He didn't have to beat him up like that, I thought. He's just a helpless old drunk.

A police car drove up. Another cop got out and the two of them rolled the drunk to the curb and hauled him like a sack of potatoes into the back seat and drove off.

A man muttered: "Damn cops, you can never find them when you want one but they's always around to beat up a drunk."

It was true, I thought. Last week when a guy from the Ebony Earls tangled with a Harlem Raider there wasn't a cop in sight until those boys had cut each other so bad they both had to be taken to Harlem Hospital.

Another man said: "We shoulda got that cop, beating that poor man like that."

"Yeah, you should of," a skinny woman said, her mouth curled up in a sneer, "but you didn't move a muscle, did you, nigger?"

"Who you callin' a nigger? I'll move a muscle and slap the shit outta you," the man said.

"Yeah," the woman answered, "you can do that all right." Sighing and shaking her head, she walked away.

Me and Sukie turned into the Regun, slid our dimes under the ticket window and got our tickets. "That cop had no call to beat up that man like that," I said.

"He shoulda whipped his raggedy ass so he could never use it no more," she said. "I hate drunks." She was mad again, just like that, puffed up and mad.

There was some boys in the lobby looking at the coming attractions, and as we passed by, one of them whispered: "Pussy, pussy, who's gonna give me some pussy?"

"Your sister," Sukie said, evil as she could be.

They fell out laughing, happy 'cause she had answered them. As I followed her down the dark aisle, I hoped the movie would make her forget about that drunk so she wouldn't be so evil. She wasn't any fun to be with when she was like this 'cause you had to be careful what you said. The least little thing would send her into a rage and she'd be ready to fight again, and I wasn't ready for that.

WEDNESDAY was the last day of school and I was pleased when I got my report card. I had four A's, two B pluses, and one C for tardiness.

Sterling was graduating from Cooper Junior High tomorrow afternoon and we was all gonna go, but wouldn't you know he had to start acting up?

That night we was in the dining room and Mother was on her knees in front of Sterling, trying to pin up the cuffs on the pants he had on, which came down over his shoe tops. The seat of the pants hung way down past his skinny behind and the sleeves of the jacket were so long his fingertips didn't even show.

"I won't go," Sterling said. "I won't wear no dead man's suit to my graduation."

"You'll go and you'll wear that suit or I'll whip your butt," Daddy yelled. "Who do you think you're talking to in that way? You suddenly so grown up you can talk to me and your mother like that?"

Daddy had bought the suit from the pawnshop. It was a good buy he said because its owner had died and the pawnbroker was letting it go for half price because it had a little bullet hole over the right pocket.

"Don't talk about not going to your own graduation, Sterling," Mother said, her mouth full of pins. "You the first one in this family ever to graduate. Ain't I always said you'd be the salvation of us all? This suit don't look too bad, do it, Francie? And when I put a tuck in the waist, and turn up the cuffs a bit . . ."

Sterling was almost in tears.

Daddy's voice softened. "Your mother sews real good, Sterling. When she gets through that suit will fit you fine. And she'll patch up that bullet hole, too. When I was a boy I didn't have a suit where the coat matched the pants until I was twenty-one and had to buy it myself. If only that last figure had been a one today I could have bought you a new suit."

Sterling pulled away from Mother and tore at the pants until they dropped to his feet. He stood there in his B.V.D.'s looking more naked than if he had no clothes on at all, screaming: "I ain't going to wear a dead man's suit to my graduation." He jumped over the pants and ran to his room.

I expected Daddy to charge after him and slam him up against the wall 'cause sassy as he was, Sterling had never defied Daddy like that before. But Daddy just looked at Mother and shrugged. "He'll be all right in the morning, Henrietta. Go on and fix the suit."

But in the morning Sterling was just as stubborn. He looked Daddy straight in the eye and told him he wasn't going.

Still Daddy didn't whip him. "It's your graduation," he said, "suit yourself," and he left to pick up his numbers.

Mother put on a clean housedress and headed for the door. "Sterling, you stay right here until I get back," she said, and left.

I followed Sterling to his room. "I wanna go to your graduation. How come you gotta mess up?"

"Get out of here before I punch you in the nose." He pushed me out of the room and slammed the door.

Mother came home shortly after twelve, carrying a big box. She marched into Sterling's room and dropped it on his bed.

"Put these on," she said, "and hurry now. I want to get a good seat up front."

Inside the box was a brand-new knickers suit, a white shirt, and tie and socks to match.

"You'll have to wear your old sneakers," Mother apologized.

Sterling jumped up and hugged Mother. She wriggled out of his embrace. "Go on now, Sterling, and get dressed before we be late. Francie, if you're going with us come on now and let me braid your hair, and wear your plaid skirt."

We didn't hear Daddy come in until he said: "What's all the excitement about?"

Mother told him in a rush. "I walked uptown to Hazel's and borrowed some money from her and bought Sterling a new suit. Good thing today is Thursday and she was home."

Daddy looked from Mother to the clothes on the bed. "And how we gonna pay Hazel back?"

"Same way we *been* paying her back," Mother snapped. "We ain't been worrying about that before, so don't start now. You goin' with us to the graduation?"

Daddy took his time answering. Finally he said: "Of course, I'm goin'." He turned to me. "Francie, when you gonna get your hair combed, it looks a mess. We don't want to be late waiting on you."

It was a good day after that. Sterling won a medal for high grades and Daddy was so proud he swelled up to twice his size and he was big enough already. Junior came to the graduation, too. He was late, but he got there.

That night the Caldwells and Mrs. Maceo came over to see Sterling's medal and Daddy played the piano and we sang the old songs and had a good time.

I was in bed almost asleep when I heard Daddy get up in the middle of the night. A few minutes later, half-dressed, he came to the front door with the suit he'd bought from the pawnbroker stuffed into a paper bag, one sleeve dangling from it.

"Where you goin', Daddy," I asked. "What you gonna do with that suit?"

"Take it down to the basement and burn it," he said, and closed the door gently behind him.

FIVE

IT was after ten o'clock but too hot to sleep so we were up on the roof searching for a cool breeze. My mother and Mrs. Caldwell were sitting on the divider between their two roofs talking to Sonny's grandmother, Mrs. Taylor. Mrs. Caldwell was holding Elizabeth's baby, a boy, while Lil Robert, five, and David, three, played at her feet.

Maude and her sister Rebecca and me were lying on the rise of the roof looking over the edge and chewing tar, which was supposed to keep your teeth white.

Rebecca was pretty, with those flashing West Indian eyes and a mouth always laughing. She was my good friend, too, although Daddy didn't like me hanging out with her too much because he said she was too old for me. She was sixteen. Daddy was afraid she might tell me something about boys, but she never did, nobody did except Sukie and that wasn't much. Sometimes I thought I must be the dumbest girl in Harlem.

I saw Sonny downstairs crossing the street and got the shivers. He was sixteen, too, strange and unsmiling, and every time I saw him now I remembered how he had

thrown his grandma's cat over the roof. I wondered if Mrs.
Taylor had whipped his behind for doing that.

"Rebecca, you think Mrs. Taylor whipped Sonny for
throwing her cat off the roof?"

"You kiddin'?" Rebecca turned her bright eyes on me.
"That boy never gets a lickin' and it's a shame because he
could be so good lookin' if some of that evil was knocked
out of him."

Rebecca got along good with boys, jiving and laughing
with them all the time in an easy way I envied. I don't think
boys liked me much, but I didn't care since I didn't like
them either and they was mostly going to end up in Sing
Sing anyhow like Daddy was always saying, especially that
Sonny, I thought. His grandmother, Mrs. Taylor, was nice,
though, dumpy and wide like most mothers, but with snow-
white hair.

"I got on relief last month," she was saying, "because I
just can't do housework no more. My rheumatism, you
know."

My mother sighed. "Lord knows I'd like to get on but my
husband just won't hear of it."

"Them men," Mrs. Caldwell said, shifting the baby to
her other hip. "Mr. Caldwell was the same way, God rest
him. Rather see these kids starve than ask somebody for a
dime. Robert's like that, too."

Mother grunted. I don't think she liked the way Robert
moved in with Mrs. Caldwell and then acted so snotty all
the time, even complaining that his mother-in-law and her
three daughters was gonna spoil his sons, and him not
working, mind you, while his wife was breaking her back in
that laundry.

Mother had told Daddy just last night: "If Robert don't
like living there, why don't he move?"

"Because he's got to help Mrs. Caldwell with her rent, that's why," Daddy said.

"Humph," Mother said, "it wasn't Mrs. Caldwell got all her furniture set out on the street. And it's a shame how Elizabeth used to never have milk for her kids but Robert kept gas in that car so he could ride around Harlem like a big shot."

"A man's got to have something like that car," Daddy said, "so he knows he's a man."

"I thought making all them babies would have told him that," Mother said, getting in the last word.

Mrs. Caldwell was saying now that she didn't care how Robert felt about it, she was applying for relief, too, and if he didn't like it he could stop hanging around with all those politicians and find himself a job.

"Y'all hear about Mrs. Petrie?" Mrs. Taylor asked. "Poor thing has another one in the oven."

Mrs. Petrie was the Twins' mother.

"How many does that make?" Mrs. Caldwell asked.

"Nine," my mother said.

"Them Catholics and that rhythm system gonna bust that oven wide open one of these days," Mrs. Taylor said. They all laughed.

"What's the rhythm system, Rebecca?" I asked.

She just giggled and looked silly so I knew it had something to do with lovemaking that grownups were always whispering about. Like I said, Daddy didn't have to worry about me learning anything from Rebecca because she never told me nothing. Well, whatever the rhythm system was the Petries had it down pat 'cause they had a brand-new baby each and every year.

FIVE fourteen finally played and not a minute too soon.

"Somebody kick me," Daddy demanded, "kick me for being a damn fool. If I had just kept that dollar on five fourteen we'd be rich tonight. Did I tell you I was playing that number because Francie dreamt a catfish bit her? Then just night before last I dreamt about my mother and switched that dollar to nine sixty-nine which plays for the dead. Somebody give me a good, swift kick in the behind."

Daddy was sitting on the piano bench, his back against the piano, facing our neighbors who had heard through the grapevine that Daddy had hit his number for a quarter and also the boleta, and had come over to help us celebrate. Mother caught it, too, for ten cents straight and thirty cents combination. Altogether they collected a fortune, almost three hundred dollars.

Mrs. Maceo was sitting in the big chair by the window frowning at her husband draped in a corner drinking himself red-eyed on King Kong. She shook her head at him in disgust, but Papa Dan ignored her, his yellow face beaming with his usual grin.

Mrs. Maceo turned toward Daddy. "The same thing happened to me last week, Mr. Coffin. You all remember that six forty-two played last Tuesday. I'd been playing that number for a month because I dreamed I was back home in Georgia planting sweet potatoes in the backyard. Madame Zora's dream book gives six forty-two for potatoes, and that same day, first thing I saw in the morning was a car with that number on its license plate. I loaded up on it. Threw my money away on that stupid number for a whole month and then dropped it two days before it came out."

"I know what you mean," Slim Jim said. "I missed my main number that same way last month and I'd been playing it for two dollars straight." Slim Jim was working for Jocko now, ever since he got out of jail a few weeks ago.

Then Mrs. Taylor and everybody else told how they, too, had messed up on their numbers.

Papa Dan belched in his corner and Sukie mumbled something under her breath which I didn't catch. We were sitting on the floor with Maude and Rebecca eating ice cream and cake and sipping that punch Mother had made. Daddy had bought two quarts of vanilla and strawberry for us and a big crock of King Kong for the grownups, though he didn't drink himself, but nobody was drinking it except Papa Dan and Slim Jim. Most of the women were eating up our cake.

"Whatcha gonna get new?" Sukie asked me.

"A pair of shoes for Sunday and a yellow dress I saw in Woolworth's basement."

"I'll wash and straighten your hair tomorrow," Rebecca offered, "a late birthday present."

"Thank you, Rebecca." My twelfth birthday had been last week. Mother had given me a dime and Daddy a quarter and now I was gonna get some new clothes, too. I smiled at Sukie, glad that we were best friends again and sorry that when I had that thirty-five cents last week I kept it a secret from her. She always shared the money she sneaked out of her mother's purse with me, and I decided then and there that I wouldn't hold out on her no more. Starting next week.

The Twins and their parents came in, Mrs. Petrie's stomach marching ahead of her as usual. Each of the Twins had a smaller child by the hand, a girl and a boy about a year apart, one coffee-brown and the other very black. All of the Petrie children were a different color. Mrs. Petrie was fair and her husband dark and they seemed bent on having a baby every color in between. The Twins were round and yellow, like a butterball, and they didn't seem to mind that wherever they went they had to cart some of the younger ones with them. Mother went in the kitchen and brought them all back a dish of ice cream.

"Stop that dribbling," one Twin told her little sister, and wiped the child's mouth with the back of her hand.

"You want some more ice cream?" I asked Rebecca.

"No, but I think I'll go get some more punch."

I walked back to the kitchen with her and as soon as we got there I knew why she liked that punch so much. The boys were standing in a circle around that big dishpan Mother had made the punch in and James Junior was sparking it with King Kong. Sterling and Vallie were watching him, together with Sonny and some other boys from Madison Avenue. That tall black one with the curly hair was Luke Washington, I thought, and the boy that looked just like him was probably his younger brother. I had heard that they both belonged to the Ebony Earls.

Rebecca grinned at Junior. "Mr. Punch Man, what you got for me?" She held out her cup and Junior smiled back at her as he dipped it in the pan. She jive-talked with the boys and stood there sipping that punch like she didn't know it had King Kong in it and I thought, if her mother saw her standin' there drinkin' that stuff she'd slap her up side her head. King Kong was homemade gin and Daddy said the niggers acted like they didn't know Prohibition was over 'cause they were still brewing their own.

I got a cup and handed it to Junior and he was filling it up when old Sterling said to me: "And just what do you think you're doing?"

"Getting me some punch. What does it look like I'm doing?"

He pointed to the milk bucket on the sink which had

some straight punch in it. "Drink that," he said, taking the cup out of my hand and emptying it back into the pan.

"I don't want none then," I said.

Rebecca was smoking that bamboo straw we made baskets with at the playground and passing it around to the others. I smoked straw, too, but I didn't dare do it now with Sterling watching. He was the strangest brother a girl ever had, always shouting and punching me when I made him mad, but never letting me have any fun.

"Your sister's growing up, Sterling," Sonny said, a cigarette dangling from his lips. "You oughta let her have a little sip."

All eyes turned on me and I felt stupid and mad at Sterling for treating me like a kid in front of everybody.

"She ain't that grown," he said.

"Well, she did grow some," Vallie said. "That's the word for Francie. Grew-some." They all fell out laughing, but it was Sonny, staring at me from under half-closed lids, that ran me out of there back up to the front room.

Elizabeth was sitting on the couch looking wistfully at the door. Daddy had just told her she was as pretty as a black queen of the Nile and it was the truth. Her eyes had gotten brighter and she laughed, showing her dimples. She was the prettiest of all the Caldwell girls and nice with it, too. She glanced at the door again and I knew she was hoping her husband Robert would come home and come over. But even if he came home he wasn't coming over here, I knew. He didn't have much to do with any of us, although he talked to Daddy all the time through the dining-room window about the Scottsboro boys and Ethiopia and stuff like that. Robert didn't seem to like nobody but Daddy, and Elizabeth, too, I guess.

Mr. Edwards, our sad-faced janitor, perched himself on the arm of our sofa, which was none too steady to begin with, and began talking to Elizabeth who soon had him laughing. I was glad about that because Mr. Edwards didn't laugh much since he lost his wife last year.

I guess it's different to lose somebody you love in death, like when we buried Mr. Caldwell last year. Everybody cried and Mrs. Caldwell held up very well until they threw the dirt on top of the casket at the cemetery. Then she howled like a banshee. But afterward we could talk about Mr. Caldwell and remember his funny West Indian ways and laugh at how he used to lock his children out if they weren't home at night by the time he told them to be.

But it wasn't like that when Mr. Edwards lost his wife. He really didn't lose her, she lost him, just upped and disappeared one night from their three-room apartment behind the stairs. His cousin Gabriel, who had come up from New Orleans to stay with them until he got settled, was gone, too. Since then everybody kept saying what a sad thing it was 'cause Mr. Edwards was such a decent man and all, although he was twenty years older than Mrs. Edwards and should have known better than to marry a high-yaller hot-blooded Creole from New Orleans. It was like a never-ending funeral with everybody clucking their teeth in sympathy whenever they saw Mr. Edwards, but being careful not to mention his wife's name, and he had shrunk so much since then that his skin folded about him now like a blanket. I liked Mr. Edwards. Whenever he sent me to the store for him he always gave me a dime. He was nice, so I was glad to see Elizabeth making him laugh for a change.

Daddy started to play the piano and everybody came in from the kitchen and crowded into the middle of the floor, doing the lindy. Then Daddy played a fox-trot and the grownups danced. Everybody sure had a good time, even Papa Dan, who had slid down in his corner to a sitting position and was snoring gently.

After everyone had gone home, Mother and Daddy sat at the dining-room table counting their money. If they counted it once they counted it a hundred times. There was something different about them tonight, some soft way they looked at each other with their eyes and smiled.

I went to bed and didn't even bother to pull the couch away from the wall, I was that happy. Let the bedbugs bite. Everybody, even those blood-sucking bugs, had to have something sometime.

WE were eating high off the hog and it sure was good to get away from that callie ham which you had to soak all night to kill the salt and then save the juice and skin to flavor beans and greens for weeks later. Nobody had to coax me now to eat those delicious pork chops and gravy and roast turkey which Daddy stuffed with his secret Geechee recipe. Daddy was a real mean cook when he had something to work with. That's what he was during the war, a cook with the navy.

It was nice, just like old times again. James Junior and Sterling came home every evening for dinner and we all ate around the dining-room table and then played checkers afterward or sang around the piano with Daddy or caught a cool breeze up on the roof and Daddy had stopped slamming doors and cursing so much.

He paid up the two months' back rent and Mother hauled us all downtown to Klein's and bought us some school clothes and two pairs of shoes each—one for Sunday and sneakers for every day—and I got that yellow ruffled dress from Woolworth's basement, too.

I even started back to music with Miss Jackson, but that only lasted two weeks 'cause by that time we was back to where we was before, just as if the big hit had never been. In fact, I think we were poorer than before. Having lived so high on the hog we naturally hated to go back to hard times. It wasn't long before the explosion came.

That Saturday Mother was at work and Daddy had already left on his rounds. I was in the kitchen cooking hominy grits and ten cents' worth of dried herrings for breakfast, stretching it out with a fishy gravy. I hated herrings and decided then and there that when I was grown I would never look another herring in the face. Mother's gravy was smooth but mine was pasty and the hominy had lumps in it. Junior ate his breakfast quietly but Sterling had to make some comment.

"Slop ain't fit for a pig," he said, looking at me with a frown and pushing his plate away.

"You're a pig," I hollered at him.

"Call me a pig again and your butt will hit this floor."

"You're a pig."

He slapped me.

"Leave her alone," James Junior said.

"He's always hitting me for nothing." I started to cry.

Sterling banged out of the house with his shoeshine box. James Junior made me blow my nose and promised me a nickel if I would stop crying. I stopped, and he left. I knew I wouldn't see him again for the rest of the day. Now that Mother was working, Junior stayed away from home more than ever.

I was still in the kitchen, scorching the rice for dinner, when the two plainclothes cops pushed past that rotten lock Daddy had never fixed and walked right in.

By the time I got to the dining room they were poking around as if they had been invited in. I knew instantly that they were cops. The oldest one was a beefy, huge man with loose jaws like a bulldog. The younger one was nervous and had quick movements like a bird.

"Where does your old man hide his numbers?" Mister Bulldog asked me, pulling open the buffet drawers.

I was so scared I couldn't speak, so I just shook my head.

Bulldog pulled the drawer out and placed it on the table. The young one sorted through it, pushing aside Mother's sewing bag and the old rags she was saving to sell to the rag man. He replaced the drawer and it jammed. I almost cried out loud. Then he gave it a shove and it closed.

They went through the other drawers in the same manner, then Bulldog went into the kitchen and began banging the pots and pans around in the cupboard.

I heard Daddy coming up the stairs and I ran toward the door, yelling: "Don't come in, Daddy. It's the cops."

Bulldog hollered: "Grab her."

The young cop swung me off my feet. I screamed and kicked, aiming for his private parts like Mother had told me to do if a man ever bothered me.

Daddy came through the door. With one long stride he was at the young cop's side. He grabbed me, at the same time pushing the cop backward.

"You all right?" Daddy asked.

I nodded. He put me down and straightened up.

"Hold it right there," Bulldog said. He was pointing a gun at Daddy's chest.

"You all got a warrant to mess up my house like this?" Daddy asked. "And stop waving that gun around. I ain't going nowhere. You're scaring my little girl to death."

Bulldog put the gun back inside his shoulder holster. "Don't need no warrant," he said. "Now hand over your numbers and come along quietly."

"You ain't got no warrant," Daddy said stubbornly.

"Search him," Bulldog ordered the young one, who approached Daddy with hesitation and went through his pockets. He pulled out an envelope. Lord, I thought, they're gonna put Daddy underneath the jail. The cop opened the envelope and pulled out an unpaid gas bill.

"The only house where we can't find a number slip," Bulldog said, "is a number runner's house. Nobody else is that careful." He reared back on his heels. "Tell you what I'm gonna do, though. I'm gonna run you in for assault and battery for pushing my partner like you did. Let's go."

I was crying loudly by this time.

"Hush," Daddy said. "You're a big girl now and you know what to do."

I nodded. He meant that after he was gone I was to take the numbers downstairs to Jocko and tell him Daddy had been arrested. He gave me a dollar to buy some meat for dinner, and he walked out the door with the two policemen following him.

I ran to the living room and climbed out onto the fire escape. A crowd had gathered downstairs. The cops pushed Daddy through them to a blue car at the curb. I watched the car until it turned the corner at 116th Street, crying, "Daddy. Daddy."

Still sniffling, I took the numbers out of the buffet downstairs to Jocko, and told him the cops had Daddy.

MOTHER and I were drinking tea at the dining-room table, very silent and blue, when Daddy returned home around ten that night. Sterling was in his room, but Junior hadn't been seen since he had left in the morning, and that worried Daddy more than his arrest.

"Damn cops," he muttered as he sat down heavily. They hadn't found any numbers on him when he came upstairs because Mr. Edwards had met him on the stoop and had warned him that two strange white men were lurking about. Everybody in Harlem was a lookout for the cops, said you could tell them by their flat feet.

"I thought the syndicate paid off so good that this wasn't supposed to happen," Mother said.

"There was a mess-up about the payoff," Daddy explained, "so the police made a few arrests to show who was boss. They didn't touch the big boys though, just a couple of small runners like me. Now if they really wanted to clean up the rackets they would have gone after Dutch Schultz."

"Maybe you'd better stop running numbers now before something worse happens," Mother said.

Daddy was gloomy. "The worse has happened. Jocko says they'll probably throw my case out of court. But I've got a record now. Fingerprints, the works." He looked at Mother and shook his head sadly. "How can I keep James Junior from running wild now that I've done gone and got a record?"

The silence grew. Mother finally cleared her throat and said: "I'm sorry this happened now because . . . well, I've got to tell you sometime and it might as well be now."

"What?"

"If it was just you and me I wouldn't mind. We could scuffle along. But I can't even scrape together enough food for the children no more. We've got no money coming in now except for those few pennies I get from Mrs. Schwartz. Lately you've been playing back all your commission on the numbers."

"So I play all the commission back. I guess you don't help, huh?"

"Yes, I do. And when I hit for two cents last week all of my money went to help repay what you owe Jocko."

"All right. All right. I'll give you back your damn twelve dollars."

"It's not that, Adam. It's having nothing coming in steady I can count on."

"All I'm trying to do is hit a big one again," Daddy said. "Those two-cent hits of yours ain't gonna make it. Nine thirty-six almost played today and I had two dollars on it. Lord, how I prayed that last figure would be a six and out pops another damned nine. We almost had us twelve hundred dollars, baby. That's all I'm trying to do. Hit us a big one."

"We can't wait until you hit a big one," Mother said, her voice cracking. She took a big breath and spoke quickly as if she had memorized the words. "I went to the relief place yesterday and put in an application. The social worker will be here Monday to talk to you."

Daddy jumped to his feet with surprising speed. The muscles in his neck bunched up and he opened his mouth but no words came. He looked like he was strangling.

Mother winced as if the sight of him hurt her. "Your pride won't feed these children," she said quietly.

Oh, Lord, I thought, as Daddy raised his hand, he's going to hit her, something he'd never done before. But he snatched up my cup instead and hurled it with all his might against the wall. It exploded into bits as he roared:

"I'm a motherfucking man. Why can't you understand that?"

I whimpered, but Mother didn't move. Then Daddy was gone, the front door slamming shut behind him.

The walls of the room were falling down on me. I had to get out of there. I jumped up and ran toward the door. Sterling came out of his room, and as I stumbled down the stairs I heard him yelling at me to come back.

I didn't stop running until I reached 115th Street and only then because I was out of breath. I was surprised to discover that my face was wet with tears.

At 114th Street a street speaker, standing on top of a ladder with a small American flag stuck in one rung, was jabbering away at a small crowd in front of him. He was West Indian, black and runty, his face purple with sweat.

"God made you black and he didn't make a mistake," the speaker shouted. "That's what Marcus Garvey said and times haven't changed. We still need a country of our own. Black people should not be encouraged to remain in the white man's land. Do you want to be a slave forever?" He glared at the crowd which stared back at him with indifference.

I moved on. These street speakers, mostly West Indians, were crazy, I thought. Who wanted to go back to Africa? Didn't we have enough trouble right here? A mounted policeman rode up and yelled at the crowd to break it up.

The next block was jammed with Puerto Ricans babbling away in Spanish, just like it was high noon instead of midnight. It was depressing, like stepping into another world and not knowing what anybody was talking about.

I walked to 110th Street and looked across Central Park at the lights twinkling in the skyscrapers. That was another world, too, all those lights way over there and this spooky park standing between us. But what good would those lights do me anyway? I bet they didn't even allow colored in those big buildings.

I turned around and started for home, creeping along,

'cause I didn't care if I never got there. I had been searching for him all the time, in every black and brown face, not really knowing I had been looking. Daddy, Daddy. Where are you? And when I got home, I knew he wouldn't be there either.

He wasn't.

SIX

THE first thing Sunday morning when I went into the bathroom I saw blood in my bloomers. I stared at it in disbelief for a moment and then started to holler: "Mother, Mother. I'm bleeding."

Mother came running. "Shut up that screaming, Francie. You ain't dying. You're just starting your period. Wait, I'll get you a clean rag."

I had heard about this, that when you was twelve you started to bleed every month, but nobody had given me any more details and I had halfway forgotten about it. Now Mother would have to tell me everything.

She returned with a torn piece of sheet and two safety pins. She folded the rag into a pad and slipped it between my legs, pinning the ends to my undershirt.

"Guess I'll have to buy you a brassiere, too," she said.

I stuck out my chest proudly. I had noticed lately that I wasn't so flat anymore.

"Francie, this means you're growing up."

"Yes, Mother." I looked up at her and waited.

Her eyes met mine. "It means . . ." she hesitated. Her

eyes dropped and her voice became crisp. "It means don't let no boys mess around with you. Understand?"

"Yes, Mother."

"Change this pad every couple of hours. There's an old raggedy sheet in the closet I'll tear up for you to use. Understand?"

"Yes, Mother."

Then she was gone, but I didn't understand any more about the period now than I had before, and what did messing around with boys have to do with it?

That night everybody was home and we sat around in the living room. Junior and Sterling were beating each other at checkers and Daddy was playing the piano.

Mother was sewing on a nineteenth-century coat her Jewish lady had given to her for me. It had leg-of-mutton sleeves, it was that old, and I swore I wouldn't wear it. Mother said it was good wool, and she had dug up a piece of fur from the trunk—saved from some other hand-me-down-special—and she was sewing it on the collar. This ratty fur collar was supposed to make the coat more glamorous to me. My protests were loud but useless. We all knew that when the wind got to whipping around those corners I'd be glad to put that coat on to keep my butt from freezing.

Suddenly Daddy swung around on the piano stool. "Y'all listen to me," he said. "The social worker is gonna interview us tomorrow so we can get on relief. Now this ain't nothing to be ashamed of. People all over the country are catching hell, same as we are and . . . well, what I want to say is never forget where you come from."

Sterling groaned and Daddy shot him a threatening look. We knew what was coming. Daddy was going to tell us again about our great-great-grandmother Yoruba. We had heard this story before, and to tell the truth, none of us believed it much, not even Mother.

I looked at her to exchange a wink like we usually did when Daddy got to talking about Yoruba, but she was looking at Daddy now with something like sorrow in her eyes. I knew it was no time to be winking and laughing at Daddy's stories.

"Your great-great-grandmother Yoruba was the only daughter of Danakil, the tribal king of Madagascar," Daddy began.

"How many greats was that again?" Sterling asked.

Daddy usually rose to the bait going into lengthy detail as to who begat who until we were all laughing and cracking up about our energetic ancestors who sure knew how to begat. But tonight he wasn't in a laughing mood.

"To be exact," he said, "she was my mother's grandmother, so you figure it out."

According to the story, Danakil had outfitted Yoruba with a trunkful of gold and sent her to England to be educated.

Richard Sommers, the son of a Charleston planter, was in England on business and fell madly in love with beautiful Yoruba. He married her and took her home with him. Yoruba was a proud spitfire of a woman and refused to allow her spirit to be crushed by her in-laws' scorn. She and Richard started a rice mill in Charleston (with her gold) and she bore him four children. When Richard died, the white Sommers wouldn't even bury him in the family graveyard or have anything to do with his colored family, but they did take over the mill, which is still thriving down there.

"What I'm trying to tell you," Daddy said, "is you should be proud to be Yoruba's children. That's what my mother told us down there in Bip. 'Don't take nothing from these crackers,' she used to say, ' 'cause you're no piece of dirt with nothing to be proud of, you're one of Yoruba's children.' "

Daddy's voice trailed off as though he had forgotten his lines. The silence grew gloomy.

"Tell us about your father, Daddy," I said, hoping this might cheer him up.

Daddy began to speak, his voice still listless. His father's father was a runaway slave who lived in the swamps for seven years eating roots and berries and things, and maybe his wife sneaked him some food sometime from the big house, I don't know, but he did have a wife 'cause she had a baby boy just at the time the Civil War started. Anyway, they was escaping in a rowboat one night with a group of other slaves to the Union side. Just as they were gliding past the enemy lines on shore, the baby started to cry. His mother rocked him frantically, patting his little back, kissing his little face, but he wailed on.

"Throw that baby overboard," the leader of the rowboat commanded, "he'll get us all killed."

The baby screamed loudly. With desperate haste the mother ripped her dress open and pushed her breast into the baby's mouth. He gurgled, sputtered, and then became still. The boat glided past the Confederate post on shore and the slaves reached the Union lines safely.

That baby, Daddy's father, grew up to be captain of a fishing boat. During a hurricane off the Charleston harbor his boat capsized and he and all eight of his men were drowned. Their bodies were never recovered.

"Your grandfather was a fearless captain, who went down with his ship," Daddy said, his voice growing stronger. "See that you don't forget it. Now times ain't always gonna be like this, and when the breaks come you gotta be prepared to take them. That's why me and your mother want you to stay in school and get a good education. Both of us only went to the fifth grade down south but you all got a better chance up here in the north. James Junior, you listening to me?"

"Yes, Daddy, I'm listening."

Daddy turned to stare at him. "What's this I hear about Sonny peeing in the classroom just before school let out? I just heard about it."

"He asked the teacher could he leave the room," Junior said, "and the teacher said no, so . . ."

"So he just stood up and pissed in a corner, huh?"

"Yeah, Daddy, that's just what he did." Junior giggled.

"Them boys are so bad the teacher spends most of her time just trying to keep order," Sterling said, frowning at Junior as if the whole mess was his fault. Junior stopped giggling.

Daddy shook his head in dismay. "You better prepare yourself for the future, I'm warning you. Times gonna get better and you ain't gonna be ready."

"Y'all better listen to your father," Mother said.

"I'm listenin'," I said. "I like school."

"You're a girl," Sterling said, siding with Junior now. "You don't know from nothing."

"I do so."

"Okay," Daddy interrupted, "enough of that. I just want you to know we got a past to be proud of." He added softly, defiantly, "Relief ain't nothing to be ashamed of."

SHE was in her early twenties, high-chested and high yaller and I hated her on sight. She thought she was cute. Besides being a social worker she also sang in Abyssinian Baptist Choir.

We were always taught to address our elders with respect, but Miss Peters sat here in our dining room calling my parents by their first names, making me madder by the minute.

"Do you have any insurance, Adam?" she asked Daddy.

"Metropolitan Life on all of us," Daddy answered.

"And what is the premium?"

"Ten cents a week each."

"Do you have any other kind of insurance?"

"I got endowment policies on all the kids," Daddy said proudly. "A thousand dollars for their college education. Took it out on them the day they was born."

"You will have to sell them."

"I will have to what?"

Miss Peters wore glasses which hung on by pinching her nose. Now she took them off and looked at Daddy as if her direct stare would help him get the message.

"You can keep the life insurance policies, Adam, but the endowment policies have a cash value. They must be surrendered and the cash realized. You can't expect us to support you when you have property that can be converted to cash."

She put the glasses back on her nose. Daddy started to protest but she cut him off rudely with another question.

A few minutes later she left and Daddy was hollering: "That ain't her goddamned money she's givin' out, you know. That ain't her money. And she's got the nerve to sing in your church choir." He looked at Mother pained. "Is that Christian behavior? Thank God I'm an atheist."

"Your mother would turn over in her grave if she heard you denying God like that," Mother said.

"Then she'll be turning from now till Gabriel blows on

his horn. And don't change the subject. I ain't selling those policies, you hear? I ain't selling them."

But Daddy did sell them and we got on relief for a hot second in the first battle of a long war with the high and mighty Miss Peters whom we promptly nicknamed Madame Queen.

PAPA Dan was dead. He had laid out drunk all night behind the stairs and caught pneumonia. He died so fast in Harlem Hospital that the only people who got a chance to visit him was Mrs. Maceo and my mother, who went with her.

Everybody, though, turned out for his services at the new funeral parlor across the street next to the grocery store. The little storefront with its folding chairs was packed. At first Sukie said she wasn't going but her mother said she would knock her into the grave they had dug for her daddy if she gave her any more lip.

At the services I sat with Mother and Daddy a few rows behind Sukie and when the minister said what a devoted husband and father our dearly departed brother had been, I thought Sukie would go out of her mind with grief, she cried that hard.

"He's gone to his just reward," the minister said, his voice trembling, "a good man, a good man."

You almost couldn't hear him over Sukie's sobs, and her carrying on so set everybody else to wailing and shrieking, including me.

China Doll and her mother hugged each other and spoke for the first time in years, and this seemed to make poor Sukie cry even harder, and everybody else, too. It sure was a good funeral.

REBECCA didn't want to go. She was ashamed to be seen in the street lugging that shopping bag filled with prunes, butter, and the gold-can jive the relief people were handing out.

"Let's go early in the morning," she told me.

"The place don't open until nine, Becky."

"Let's be at the door then, Francie. I tell you what I'll do. I'll take you to the movies tomorrow night and pay your way. Ken Maynard's playing. Ask your mother if you can go."

We were talking through the dining-room window. It was too hot to sleep and we had just come down from the roof. It was after twelve, but the midnight heat was just as stifling as the noonday sun. I turned away from the window and went to find Mother who was in the front room.

"Mother, can I go to the show with Becky tomorrow night?"

"Francie, come on and let's pull your bed away from the wall, and you get on in it. How do I know what you can do tomorrow night? Ask your father when he comes home."

"Where is he?"

"Playing poker, I expect." She mumbled something under her breath. They had argued last week about Daddy staying out so late every night playing cards. Daddy said he won most of the time so what was she griping about. Mother answered she never saw no extra money and God knows they needed every dime they could lay their hands on instead of throwing it away on cards.

I really didn't want to ask Daddy about going to the movies with Rebecca because he always said she was too old for me to be hanging around with, so I asked Mother again, and she said yes and to come on now and get to bed.

The next morning Becky and I were first in line at the re-

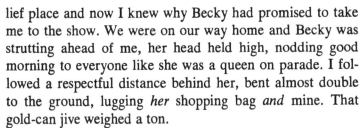

lief place and now I knew why Becky had promised to take me to the show. We were on our way home and Becky was strutting ahead of me, her head held high, nodding good morning to everyone like she was a queen on parade. I followed a respectful distance behind her, bent almost double to the ground, lugging *her* shopping bag *and* mine. That gold-can jive weighed a ton.

Becky stopped at 119th Street to talk to three boys sitting on the stoop, who were up suspiciously early. I stopped, too, putting down the shopping bags and wiping my sweating palms. Rebecca sent a fierce look in my direction and I grabbed up the bags and stumbled on.

"Morning, Becky," I said as I passed her.

"Hello, Francie. Where you been so early?"

Without waiting for an answer she turned back to the boys and they all burst out laughing. I trudged on. Damn if the movies was worth all this shit.

By the time I got inside my hallway, Becky caught up with me and took her shopping bag.

"You didn't have to pretend as if you barely knew me," I complained as we continued up the stairs together.

"Don't be silly. I spoke to you, didn't I?"

"We still going to the movies tonight?"

"Maybe. That Duke, the one I was talking to, asked me to go to the Rennie with him. There's a barn dance tonight."

"Becky. You promised."

"Okay, we'll go early, about three o'clock and maybe Mama will still let me go to the dance. Watch me over the roof."

We climbed up the last flight and went through the roof door and I watched her as she crossed over the divider separating our two houses and pulled open her door.

"You be ready by three o'clock," she said, "and if you come over early I'll curl your hair."

"I'll be over early," I yelled as she disappeared through the door. That Becky sure was handy with a curling iron. I was glad she was my friend. I don't care what Daddy said.

I took the shopping bag into the kitchen and Mother put the food on the drainboard, looking rather hard at the canned meat wrapped so gaily in its yellow paper. I knew what she was thinking, what recipe would she use to doctor it up with this time?

The labels on the cans read "Choice Cuts of Beef," but everybody in Harlem swore it was really horsemeat, and no matter how our mothers sliced it, baked it, or stewed it, nobody would eat the mess, which we named the gold-can jive.

Mrs. Maceo had come up with a southern recipe, deep fried in batter, but her family wouldn't even break the crust. Mrs. Caldwell added plantains for a West Indian specialty, but her kids said it smelled funky. My mother baked it with tomatoes and green peppers, but none of us would touch it, except Daddy, who we jokingly called the human garbage can. Finally, our mothers stopped exchanging those delicious recipes and that gold-can jive started stacking up in everybody's cupboards, making the shelves buckle.

Rebecca didn't take me to the movies that afternoon after all. Her mother asked her if she was losing her mind. It was either the movies *or* the barn dance. Naturally Becky chose the dance, but she gave me a dime for the movies, so I wasn't mad at her. I had been waiting for Becky all day to make up her mind, so I got to the movies just before the prices changed at five o'clock.

I hadn't been there ten minutes before that fat little white man with the bald head who used to try to get me to come up on the roof slid into the seat next to me. I had to giggle. He sure was crazy about Westerns. Almost every time I came to the show by myself he would sit next to me, hand me a dime, and start feeling me under my skirt. We never said a word to each other, he would just hand me the money and start feeling.

I never let him get his hands too far inside my bloomers, though. By the time he worked his way up inside the elastic leg and got too close, I would shift my butt and he would have to start all over again, or I would change my seat.

Today, though, I guess I got too carried away with the picture and almost forgot all about him. Ken Maynard was my favorite. He and the rangers had just butchered a whole tribe of Indians to rescue this girl Ken Maynard liked, and now, in the moonlight, in his shy, sweet way, he was about to kiss her.

I felt a stirring in my stomach. Then I realized that this fat little man had gotten his fingers all the way inside me. I was throbbing down there like a drum. I squirmed. My legs opened wider, and his fingers moved higher. My flesh seemed to rush to meet him. I groaned. I was caving in, all of my insides straining toward that center where his fingers were making me melt. My God. I was on fire.

His hand touched a raw nerve and a streak of pain ripped through me. I snapped my legs shut, imprisoning his fingers. Violently, I tore his hand away and flung it back at him. I stood up, and stumbled down the aisle and into the street.

I went flying down 116th Street, that strange throbbing between my legs. It was wet down there. I could feel it collecting in my bloomers. I turned the corner at Fifth Avenue and raced home.

Mother was in her bedroom talking to Mrs. Caldwell through the window. I tiptoed into the bathroom and pulled down my bloomers with shaking fingers. It was wet all right. Goopy. Mother would kill me. I pulled off the bloomers and dabbed at the goop with a wet washcloth.

Why had I felt like that? That man was always following me because he knew he could make me feel that way. The memory of my opening my legs wider filled me with shame. That's the way those girls acted in the *True Confessions* magazines, and they always came to a bad end. When I read about them kissing and messing around, it always made me tingle down there—that's why I read that stuff—but it was nothing like when that man was feeling me. If Mother saw these dirty pants she'd know I'd been doing something bad and she'd whip me with the thick end of the razor strop.

I scrubbed my bloomers harder. The fear came that somehow my guilt would show. Then I had a stupid thought: Maybe that's the way babies were made. My mind dashed about madly but I made it stop. I knew good and well you had to fuck to make a baby. Sukie said they put their thing inside you. It was a nasty, filthy thing to do, and I decided then and there that no man was ever going to put his thing inside me.

When I went to bed that night I couldn't sleep. I scratched and smashed bedbugs by the hundreds and finally gave in to my latest daydream.

I was standing downstairs on the stoop and he came thundering down Fifth Avenue on his great white horse. Ken Maynard. I ran out into the street and without even slowing up, he bent down and swooped me up in his arms, setting me on the saddle behind him. I took one last look at

the bell tower in Mt. Morris Park before we rode out of
Harlem and into the sunset.

Just before I fell asleep, the memory of that man's hand
inside me knotted up my stomach again, and I wondered
sadly if I was gonna come to a bad end.

SEVEN

AFTER Labor Day we went back to school, that is Sterling and I did, James Junior went back to playing hooky. Sterling was going downtown to high school, grumbling that all the white kids wore better clothes than he did and had long pants while he was still knocking about in his knickers. Daddy told him he should have appreciated that nice suit with the long pants he got him from the pawnshop because God knows when he'd get the money to buy him another one.

We didn't have any money at all, and that was the truth. When we got our relief check each month all we did was take it across the street to Mr. Burnett, the West Indian grocer, and pay him what we owed. This left us with nothing so the next day we started buying on credit again. Daddy said we'd never get out the hole that way.

It got so I hated to go across the street to Mr. Burnett's with our credit book clutched in my hand 'cause his wife would look at you cross-eyed after you ordered all those bags of groceries then held out that book instead of money. And their snotty little daughter, Yolanda, was worse yet. It got so bad that both me and Rebecca hated to set foot in that store and she would cry when her mother sent her there to buy something on credit.

Today I was in the kitchen shelling some peas when Mother gave me a list of things to get from Mr. Burnett and handed me the credit book. I tried to pull a Rebecca by poking out my mouth and saying I didn't want to go. Mother looked at me like I was crazy.

"Don't give me no lip, Francie. Take that book across the street and get those groceries or I'll blister your behind again with the thick end of the strop."

"Yes, Mother."

"And get three kaiser rolls from the baker's." She handed me a nickel.

I left in a hurry, but sat down on the fourth landing to think over how bad things were getting. Yesterday was the first time in my life I had been whipped with the thick end of the strop and here Mother was threatening to do it again. I needed a nickel so bad yesterday that when I saw Mr. Edwards and he didn't offer me one I sort of suggested it to him. He gave me a dime, then squealed to Mother soon's she came home from work.

The first thing Mother said to me when she came through the door, mad as she could be, was: "Get me the razor strop." Since nobody else was there except her and me, I was worried about her asking for that strop like that.

"You gonna beat me?" I asked. "What did I do?"

"How many times I got to tell you, Francie, that if somebody got something for you they'll give it to you without you having to ask for it. Go get me the strop."

Mr. Edwards, I thought. The bastard had ratted on me. I went into the bathroom and got the strop and walked back outside. I handed it to Mother and backed away.

"I only asked him for a nickel, Mother, and it wasn't like asking a stranger." She moved toward me and I saw with horror how she was holding that strop. "You ain't gonna beat me with the thick end?" I couldn't believe it and knocked over a chair getting out of her way.

Mother kept on coming. "I ain't gonna chase you all over this room," she said, and snatched me and dragged me into her bedroom, flinging me down on the bed. I was too long legged to be put across her lap, so she sort of kneeled on my back and pulled down my bloomers with one hand, raising the strop with the other.

"I told you before and I ain't gonna tell you again. Don't beg nobody for nothing."

Each word was punctuated with a lash on my bare behind, and each lash raised a welt and a scream from me until I was hoarse.

"Don't beg nobody for nothing."

Mother beat me so long I think her arm got tired.

I had asked Mr. Edwards for that nickel so I could have fifteen cents to eat at Father Divine's 'cause all we had at home was leftover cabbage which hadn't been too tasty yesterday. The only other thing was that gold-can jive and nobody in their right mind would eat that mess. Anyway, after Mr. Edwards gave me the money, I walked up to 130th Street to get one of Father's delicious chicken dinners. Peace, it's wonderful.

Father Divine's place was in a basement apartment. I paid my fifteen cents at the door and found a seat at a round table in the middle of the room, crowded with men, women, and children, all eating silently. Some of them were Father's followers—I could tell by their nappy heads—but others were just hungry people like me.

One of Father's angels, a huge black woman dressed in a

bed sheet, brought me a plate of golden brown chicken from the kitchen. She nodded toward the bread and vegetables on the table, meaning for me to help myself. Instead of grace you had to praise Father's holy name, so I turned to the man next to me and said: "Father Divine is God, would you please pass me that plate of blackeye peas?"

When I finished eating I walked back home, skirting Mt. Morris Park. I liked the food at Father Divine's, you got plenty to eat for your fifteen cents, but I always had to come alone. Nobody would come with me, not Sukie or Rebecca or even Maude. They were ashamed of those nappy-headed angels who wouldn't straighten their hair and wore white robes and changed their names to Beloved Theresa or Sweet Morning Glory when they entered Father's kingdom.

No, I thought now, as I got up off the steps and went on downstairs to go to the store, that dinner sure wasn't worth my whipping.

Rebecca was sitting on my stoop talking to Duke from 119th Street. He was a raggedy black boy and I don't know what Rebecca saw in him.

"I don't have to go to Mr. Burnett's no more," she bragged. "I told my mother this morning I just wasn't going."

"Did she slap you up side your head?" I asked.

"No, she sent Maude instead."

There was something chilly about Maude. What I mean is she didn't get all hot and bothered about things like me and Rebecca did. Maude went with me now to get the gold-can jive and prunes from the relief office and to a church on 121st Street where we got day-old bread for five cents a loaf.

I went to the bakery first, wishing I had a younger sister to send to the store.

"Three poppy-seed rolls," I told Max who was standing behind the high counter. He was so short his pinpoint head could just be seen over the top. I looked at the cinnamon buns in the case, wishing I had a nickel to buy me some.

Max saw me looking at them and when he handed me the bag of rolls he said: "You want a cinnamon bun, Francie?"

"I don't have no more money," I said, handing him the nickel for the rolls.

He put a cinnamon bun in the bag. "Come in the back for a minute," he said.

"No, thank you," I said. "I got to go to the grocery store for my mother."

He took the cinnamon bun back.

The stingy bastard, I thought, as I crossed the street slowly, dreading every step of the way. Max shoulda given me a bun for that free feel he got last night. I'd been playing ringoleevio with the Twins and Sukie and went and hid in the telephone booth in Max's store. He had come with the broom and pretended to be sweeping in front of the booth and got himself a good feel before I was able to get out of there.

A group of boys was walking down the street and wouldn't you know they'd stop right in front of the grocery store to cut up? I moaned my bad luck. They made me feel so miserable that ordinarily to avoid passing them I'd cross the street. But there was no escaping them today.

"Skeebopadee, this skinny one's for me," the blackest boy of the bunch yelled.

I braced myself, staring straight ahead, and walked past them.

"You give me yours and I'll give you mine," another boy hollered. "I'm talking 'bout your cherry." He did a tap dance, poking out his belly at me, and the other boys broke up laughing.

I escaped into the store, but my luck was still bad. It wasn't Mr. Burnett, a jolly West Indian, behind the counter, but his fat yellow wife. And Yolanda, nine, light-skinned and plump like her mother, with long braids hanging down her back, was perched on a high stool next to the rice sack.

"Hello, Mrs. Burnett. Hello, Yolanda."

They both grunted at me. "Three pounds of rice," I read from the list, adding as Mrs. Burnett went to the five cents a pound sack, "Three pounds for ten cents." She grunted again and scooped up the cheaper rice. "Ten cents' worth of dried herrings."

"They's fifteen cents a pound."

"My mother only wants ten cents' worth." My voice was barely above a whisper.

She threw the herrings on the scale and snatched them off before I could see how much she had given me. I read the rest of the items off the list and watched as Mrs. Burnett wrote the prices on a large paper bag and added them up.

"That will be two dollars and ninety-eight cents."

I caught my breath and held out the credit book. It seemed like forever I was holding that book out and she looking at it like she never saw it before, which was silly. She saw it almost every day.

"When do you all get your relief check?" she asked.

"The first of the month, Mrs. Burnett." She knew it was the first. She knew it, she knew it. Finally, she took the book, grumbling under her breath, wrote the figure on it and threw it on top of the groceries. She pushed the bag toward me and I picked it up from the counter.

All of this time Yolanda's black button eyes were burning a hole in my back. She never played with the rest of us and I don't know why me and Rebecca let her get on our nerves. After all, she was only nine, going on ten, but she sat there on that stool, silent and snotty, making me feel that it was not only her store but her world and I had no place in it.

But being in hock to the grocer wasn't enough to make our social worker, Madame Queen, happy. The next time she came to check up on us she told Daddy he had to be making some extra money somewhere 'cause we spent more on rent and food than what the relief gave us. She was right. Daddy wasn't bringing home hardly anything from his numbers, but Mother was still working three half days for Mrs. Schwartz and Sterling brought home a couple of bucks now and then from his shoeshining.

"I ain't working, Miss Peters," Daddy told her. "How many times I have to tell you that." He was standing up straight and tall, looking down at her sitting at our dining-room table, her papers and figures spread out before her. I hoped her glasses would pinch her nose off.

"Is anybody in this household working, Adam?"

"No."

"I don't understand then how you can pay your rent and food and gas bill."

"We manages, Miss Peters."

"But where do you get the money from if no one is working?"

"We just gets it somehow."

"Then somebody *is* bringing in extra money."

"No, Miss Peters. We don't have one dime except what you all give us."

They kept at it like that for ten minutes more and I could

have slapped her yellow face for pushing Daddy into a corner like that.

When she finally left, Daddy said wearily: "They don't give you enough money to live on so you have to bootleg some kind of work, then they want to deduct that from your relief check, too. I wonder how they expect you to live. Didn't I tell you I didn't want to mess with those people?" But for once he didn't shout, seeming to be more tired than angry.

I HAD been upstairs playing jacks with Maude and was going home now, but it was too dark to go over the roof so I was running down the stairs. I stopped short when I saw Sonny on the ground floor.

"Hello, Sonny."

"Hello, Francie."

I walked slowly down the last steps.

"Come on," Sonny said, dancing around and aiming his fist at my jaw, "let's box."

I threw up my hands to protect myself and backed up. The next thing I knew we were in the shadows behind the stairs and Sonny was leaning all over me, pulling my dress up.

"I don't wanna box no more," I said. "I wanna go home."

"Let me put it in you for a minute, Francie." Then his bare flesh, hot and wet and hard, was on my thigh. "Open your legs a little, Francie."

"No." Suddenly, I was scared. I tried to dodge around him but he reached out with one arm and flung me back against the wall.

"It won't hurt, Francie." He was rubbing himself up and down against me, one hand beneath the elastic leg of my bloomers and the other at my waist trying to pull my bloomers down.

"No. I don't wanna."

Frantic now, I held on to my bloomers with both hands, but they were slowly being forced down as Sonny poked his thing at me and tried to stick it over the top of my bloomers.

I stopped struggling for a moment to get my breath. Just as my bloomers were about to slide down over my knees, I wrenched free and hauled them back up. Sonny grabbed me again.

Then we heard somebody bouncing down the stairs singing. I held my breath and Sonny stopped his jiggling, both of us listening for the front door to slam. But instead, the singing came closer. I recognized Vallie's voice just before I saw him heading for the dark under the stairs. He had on one of Rebecca's cotton dresses and he was pulling up his knickers. He took the dress off and bundled it into a ball. He was whistling now, walking toward us to hide that dress under the stairs, I thought.

Sonny buttoned up his pants, his fingers stumbling in haste, and I pulled my dress down.

"Hold your hands up higher," Sonny suddenly hollered, and went into his fighter's stance. I just stood there, scared and dumb.

"Who's that back there?" Vallie asked.

Sonny danced out into the light, shadowboxing. "Me and Francie," he said. "I was showing her how Joe Louis delivers his powerhouse upper-right cross. Pow." Sonny aimed one at Vallie's chin. Vallie ducked. Sonny laughed and shadowboxed himself right out into the vestibule. The door slammed shut behind him.

I walked toward Vallie, looking everywhere except at him.

"What was you doing behind the stairs with Sonny?" he asked.

"What?"

"He screw you?"

"You crazy or somethin'?"

"What was you doing back there with him?"

"We was boxing."

"That's what they call it now, huh?"

"I wasn't doing nothing. I don't want to ever do nothing." I started to cry.

"Aw, Francie. I'm sorry. I didn't mean . . . Francie, please. Don't cry."

He wiped my face with the dress and then he kissed me on the cheek. When I didn't move, his lips touched mine for an instant, pressing down firmly.

"You all right now?"

I nodded. "I wasn't doing nothing with Sonny. Honest I wasn't."

"I believe you, Francie. But don't let him hem you up in no dark corner anymore. He don't mean you no good. Okay?"

"Okay, Vallie."

We went outside, crossed over to my stoop, and he walked me upstairs to my door. I was hoping he would kiss me on the mouth again, I liked that, but he didn't. I listened to him galloping down the stairs and then I went on inside.

The next afternoon Rebecca and I went to the Apollo Theatre. We sat upstairs in the buzzard's roost 'cause it only cost a dime, although the sweet fumes from those skinny cigarettes the boys were smoking was so thick it gave me a headache. Ralph Cooper was the master of ceremonies and him and Butterbeans and Susie made me laugh till I hurt. The picture was good, too, Janet Gaynor and Lionel Barrymore and Stepin Fetchit in "To Carolina." Everybody laughed at Stepin Fetchit and so did I 'cause he was funny and a big movie star and making all that money, but sometimes I wished he wasn't such a shufflin', lazy nigger.

When the show was over we walked right into a riot. We had walked to Lenox Avenue and saw a crowd near 126th Street and went up there. A wooden platform was up in the street and several black and white men yelling into a microphone. There were hundreds of people milling around and a whole lot of cops swinging their billy clubs and hollering at the crowd to move on. I saw one cop rap a Negro right in the middle of his forehead and draw blood. I shuddered and turned away.

A banner over the platform said: "Welcome home Mrs. Ada Wright, Mother of Roy and Andy." We would have gone on home then except that Rebecca suddenly yelled: "Hey, that's Robert up on that platform."

I looked and sure enough it was. He grabbed the microphone and began hollering into it: "Do not disperse. We have a right to meet on our own streets."

Just then a whole row of police cars drove up. As the cops jumped out they threw something into the air.

"Tear gas," somebody yelled. "Oh, my God, they're gassing us."

The crowd, which had been pressing up against the platform, scattered. People grabbed their throats, strangling, as the air about them turned smoky.

Just then Robert saw us and shouted at me and Rebecca to get out of there. We turned and ran with the crowd. The cops were chasing us up Lenox Avenue. People upstairs on their fire escapes and hanging from their windows threw rotten fruit down on the police.

"Got one of the bastards," somebody yelled, as a banana skin fell on top of a cop's cap.

"Come on," Rebecca cried, "we'd better get out of here before they start shooting."

A soggy tomato fell at my feet. I picked it up and threw it at the nearest cop, then Rebecca and I ran down to Fifth Avenue and went home.

I told Mother about the riot and we sat in the dining room drinking tea, waiting for the boys to come home. Sterling came in first and then around midnight James Junior showed up. Mother made me go on to bed. Hours later I woke up and went into the dining room. Mother was still sitting at the table, waiting. My eyes met hers and I saw fear in them. She was waiting for Daddy and I realized for the first time that I wasn't the only one in that house who was always afraid the worse had happened.

"Go on back to bed, Francie."

"Yes, Mother."

At daybreak Daddy came home and Mother finally went to bed.

The next day the front page of the papers was full of it: "5,000 Negroes and white sympathizers rioted yesterday when detectives used tear gas bombs to disperse an unauthorized meeting staged at Lenox Avenue and 126th St. to protest the Scottsboro case."

The paper said the International Labor Defense Committee planned the meeting to welcome home Mrs. Ada Wright, mother of two of the Scottsboro boys, Roy and Andy. She had been to Alabama to see them and Harlem was welcoming her home. I stopped reading in disgust when the paper said that the police didn't use clubs or pistols against the rioters. If that wasn't a billy club that cop used on that colored man's head then I was stone-blind.

The paper also said three people were arrested, two white men and a Negro. Thank God it wasn't Robert, but his picture was in the paper up there on that platform and on account of it he lost the job he just got as a delivery boy downtown in the garment center 'cause he hadn't gone to work that day but had taken off sick.

The next night the whole courtyard could hear Robert's argument with Elizabeth. I was lying on Mother's bed and their voices rose up plain and clear in the air shaft which our bedroom windows opened on.

"How come you let those Communists make you lose your job?" Elizabeth asked.

"The Black League for Freedom ain't Communist," Robert said. "We just helped the defense committee set up the meeting."

"The papers say you all a bunch of Communists."

"Screw the papers."

"You care more about them Scottsboro boys than you do about your own sons starving right under your nose."

"They're not starving right under my nose. You're working, ain't you? Liz, I got to care what happens to black people in Alabama. Nine colored boys are condemned to die because two white sluts said they raped them. Ain't that a bitch? Can't you understand that what happens to them down south is part of what happens to us here in Harlem?"

"All I understand is I ain't gonna be working my butt off in no laundry while you're parading and marching up and down getting your picture in the papers. I just ain't gonna do it so you'd better stop losing jobs and messing around with those Communists."

"How many times I got to tell you the Black League ain't—"

"I don't care what they ain't. They ain't paying you a dime, that I know, and you laying up here like a king in my mother's house and—"

"You want me to leave your mother's house? Just keep shouting and screaming like that. You want me to leave?"

There was silence. I waited and waited for Elizabeth to answer but she never did. Finally, disgusted with waiting, I got into my own bed and fought with the bedbugs and finally fell asleep.

The next morning when I went to get Maude for school, Robert was still there and I didn't hear Elizabeth arguing with him anymore either. In fact she looked kind of silly, smiling and giggling about nothing, and I wondered what old Robert had done to make her so happy like that for a hot minute.

MR. EDWARDS hit 505 for two dollars and said he was going to New Orleans to look for his wife and his cousin, Gabriel. I was glad 'cause I wasn't mad at him anymore for making me get that beating. When I told him about it the next day he swore he hadn't meant to get me in dutch and I believed him.

But Mr. Edwards didn't get paid off on his hit. The bankers changed that last figure to a 6 when they found out that a whole mess of people in Harlem had that number. A plane had crashed the day before and its picture was in the *News* with 505 painted on one wing.

"It's a shame," Daddy said, "the way the racketeers can change a number anytime they want to as if the thousand to one odds against hitting ain't enough for them."

Mr. Edwards thought it was more than a shame. He went raving and cursing up to his collector demanding his money and got shot twice for his trouble. He died three days later in Harlem Hospital. There was no funeral because one of his relatives sent his body straightaway to New Orleans and I thought it was kinda sad for Mr. Edwards to get back home that way.

They didn't keep that man who shot Mr. Edwards in jail no time before they turned him loose. "Niggers killing niggers don't bother the police none," Daddy said. "They just don't give a damn."

With Mr. Edwards gone we didn't have a janitor and our Jewish landlord came down from Mt. Vernon and offered Daddy the janitor's job. He took it and it became our lot to pull the garbage and mop down the stairs and keep the backyard clean which was none too easy since it was simpler to throw garbage out of the window into the backyard than to wait until six o'clock when the garbage was pulled. That dumbwaiter was a filthy, slimy mess, a permanent home for cockroaches and rats, and I would just as soon open the window myself and sling the garbage out than open that dumbwaiter door.

Daddy got up at five o'clock in the morning to start the furnace in the basement before somebody started banging on the pipes for hot water, but he made James Junior and Sterling bank the fire at night, and that kept Junior a little closer to home.

We had been janitors before, a long time ago when I was four and we lived in that basement in Brooklyn with the furnace pipes standing right in the middle of every room. I remember because we were the only colored in that whole block and I used to play with a pretty little Jewish girl, Rosina, who lived up on the third floor and had a brand-new baby brother. She had the youngest, nicest parents, and her father always made us laugh by jumping into the baby's crib to read his newspaper every evening when he came home. I used to go up there just to see him do that, then he would hug us both and give us a lollipop he had hidden in his coat pocket.

Me and Rosina started kindergarten together and were best friends because while there were two or three other colored kids in our school, janitor's children, too, they didn't live near me.

Now that I think back on it, things were real nice there in Brooklyn. We had a telephone and one of those radios with earplugs and we would listen to it every evening and have a good time together and Mother didn't work and was always at home. But after we moved to Harlem we seemed to get poorer and poorer. I asked Mother once why we ever left Brooklyn and she said so Daddy could take a better job painting but it didn't turn out to be steady because of the Depression. Now, I thought, with Daddy being a janitor again maybe things would be nicer like when we used to live in Brooklyn. But that janitor's job only got us in trouble. It was on account of it that Madame Queen cut us off relief, because Daddy hadn't told her about it right away.

"But I don't receive any pay for being the janitor," Daddy told Madame Queen, "only a reduction in rent, just half, and I was going to tell you next month after we caught up. We owe most of our relief check to the grocer and I was just trying to break even before I told you."

But Madame Queen didn't believe Daddy. As good as called him a liar, and to punish us, she took us off relief. Mother told Daddy Mrs. Schwartz's sister wanted her to work part time and maybe that would help some. Daddy didn't say anything, so Mother took the job and was gone now every afternoon instead of just three times a week.

Now that she was away so much we didn't eat dinner together anymore. Junior and Sterling came home at different times and ate in the kitchen. Daddy would put on some mustard greens before he left on his rounds, and when I came home from school I would turn them off and cook a pot of rice. Daddy was a Geechee so we had rice every day. Me and that rice. It was either scorched or a soggy mess. Once Daddy looked at it with disgust. That day it was soggy.

"Why in hell don't you teach this girl to cook a decent pot of rice?" he roared at Mother.

My feelings were hurt. Mother didn't bother to answer, her silence saying louder than words that he was home all day so why didn't he teach me himself.

"You a moron or something," he turned on me, "that you can't cook a decent pot of rice?"

My tears were instant. "I measure it out just like you do, Daddy, only it gets dry while it's still raw so I add more water."

"The gas, the gas," Daddy yelled, "you've got the damn gas turned up too high. You don't boil rice, you steam it."

The sight of my tears didn't make him turn gentle as it usually did. He finished eating and banged out of the house mumbling that it was a goddamn shame a man couldn't get a decent pot of rice in his own home. I felt bad for hours 'cause Daddy seldom hollered at me, but after that I didn't cook any more soggy pots of rice.

That Saturday night I was up late because there was no school the next day. Me and Mother were home alone. She was in her bedroom figuring out the lead for Monday, Daddy had taught her his system, and I was sitting at the dining-room table reading a library book, armed with my usual supply of weapons. Tonight I had a hammer, a screwdriver, and two hairbrushes. When I heard a noise I threw the hammer toward the kitchen and the rats scurried back into their holes. When I got down to my last piece of ammunition I would give the dining room up to the rats and go on to bed. I was scared to death of those rats. They had already bitten everybody but me. They tell me that when I was a baby they had to keep me in a laundry basket on top of the dresser to protect me from those rats.

Our rats grew fat on the poison Mother spread around each week on raw potato slices, and the sulfur bombs she was always gassing us with had no effect on them whatsoever. Once they chased a cat we had right into the living-room wall and I bet that cat kept on running till he got to Brooklyn.

I had finally deserted the fairy tales at the library—more out of shame than anything else—and had discovered a row of bookcases called the Negro Section with books in it about colored people. I was reading *Home to Harlem* by Claude McKay and it was strange to discover that someone had written about these same raggedy streets I knew so well. The people in the book acted just like those clowns out there on Fifth Avenue and it was very funny and kind of sad.

But I couldn't keep my mind on the book because I was hoping James Junior would beat Daddy home so there wouldn't be another argument.

I threw the screwdriver down the hall and just then there was a loud banging on the dining-room door. Sudden noises scared me—usually it meant something terrible had happened—so I just sat there with my heart pounding, not making a move.

"What's the matter with you, Francie," Mother grumbled as she went to the door. "Can't you hear all that banging? You act more like a moron each day."

It was true. I was getting scared of everything. It was Sukie's mother, her moriney face redder than usual after her climb up to the top floor.

"Mr. Coffin home?" she asked. "Oh, Lord, Lord, Lord."

"He ain't here," Mother said. "What's the matter?"

"You better sit down, Mrs. Coffin," Mrs. Maceo said, bending her tall frame into a chair.

"No," Mother said, stiffening. "What is it?"

"They found a white man dead in a hallway around on 118th Street. That was about seven o'clock, I guess. Didn't you hear about it?"

Mother shook her head.

"Well, he was mugged to death. Didn't have no pants on when they found him." She looked at me. "How come you didn't hear about it, Francie?"

"I been upstairs all evening," I said, wondering if that was all she came to tell us. I started to relax.

"The cops just busted into that basement where the Ebony Earls holds their meetings," Mrs. Maceo said, "and they done arrested all of them boys. Holding them for murder."

I felt a curious stillness, like my heart and the world had just stopped running. Mother fell into a chair, her hand going up to her mouth in that familiar gesture she used when she laughed and exposed her toothless gums.

"James Junior?" she asked. "He arrested, too?"

Mrs. Maceo nodded. "Him and Vallie and four other boys from Madison Avenue."

"I always knew this day was coming," Mother said slowly. "I always knew I would turn a corner and run into this day, but I ain't prepared for it nohow."

The next morning his picture stared up at me from the front page of the *Daily News*. That white bald-headed man who used to hang out on my roof and follow me to the movies, he was the man Junior and Vallie were arrested for murdering.

PART II

YORUBA'S
CHILDREN

EIGHT

IT snowed all night, the first snow of the season, and in the morning the streets were a fairy wonderland—whitewashed and lovely. Even though I hated cold weather, Maude and I enjoyed the newness of the snow as we walked to school, watching the younger kids bang each other over the head with snowballs.

Nothing much was changed at school. We were still messing up in our algebra class, reading smutty love stories and dirty comics in place of *True Romances*. I was also reading *Uncle Tom's Cabin,* from the library, which made me feel black and evil toward whites. Luisa and Saralee had been left back again and were still scaring the pee out of everybody.

After school I started for home, going out of my way to walk through the park, it was just that nice a day, brisk but not too cold. The trees were so still, so quietly beautiful, their black branches bowed with a frothy icing, that I almost didn't notice that the snow I was crunching under my feet was soaking into my stockings and making my toes numb.

It was so quiet in that park, it was almost solemn. It was like that in the streets, too, everything clean and hushed under its white blanket. But I knew that in a few days the snow would be banked up in piles in the gutter and the dogs would raise one leg and let yellow streams stain it, and garbage and ashes would freeze into it, making one big mountain of filth. But now it was all new and sparkling.

The silence was broken by somebody calling my name. I looked up and there in front of me was Saralee and Luisa.

"Didn't you hear me callin' you?" Saralee asked, her bottom lip poked out.

I shook my head. She had on layers and layers of sweaters and a pair of maroon pants and was bareheaded. It's true, I thought. She does look more like a man each day. She certainly was too black and ugly with her red-headed self to be a girl.

"You think you're cute, don't you?" Saralee said.

"Naw," I answered, getting nervous. "I know I'm ugly."

"Come here and let's see just how ugly you really are," she said.

Luisa giggled. She was dressed in a big coat that looked like a live bear, and I couldn't understand why such a pretty Puerto Rican wanted to hang out all the time with that mannish Saralee. Despite the cold I could feel the sweat collecting under my armpits as I walked toward her.

She grabbed me in the collar and pulled the scarf off my head, inspecting me closely. "You're not so ugly," she grinned. I pulled away from her and her grin turned into a frown.

"Slap the shit out of her and let's get going," Luisa said. "I'm cold."

"You do and you won't slap another soul this side of the grave," a voice said. It was Sterling, making his way toward us across a field of snow which came up to his knees. Was I glad to see Sterling. He reached us and snatched me away from Saralee.

"You must be outta your mind, nigger, messin' in my business like this," Saralee said.

"The next time you say more than two words to my sister," Sterling said, "I'm gonna kick your ass all over Harlem."

I didn't see her reach for it, but suddenly there was a switchblade in Saralee's hand. The blade was wicked and long, and its shadow, stretched out on the white snow, was even longer.

"I'll take that knife away from you and slit your own throat with it," Sterling said. He took a step forward and Saralee backed up and went into a crouch, her knife hand aimed at Sterling's throat. I started to shiver.

"Say, ain't you Junior Coffin's brother?" Luisa asked. She turned to Saralee. "Junior's an Ebony Earl, one of those guys who killed that peckerwood last month."

"He didn't kill nobody," I screamed.

"Why didn't you say who you was?" Saralee asked, straightening up and snapping the knife shut. "We don't mess with no Ebony Earl's sister, man."

"Just don't mess with *my* sister," Sterling said, grabbing my hand and pulling me behind him so fast I could hardly keep up.

When we were out of earshot, I said: "He didn't kill nobody, Sterling. James Junior couldn't have done it, could he?"

"I don't think so, Francie."

"It sure is a good thing though that you happened along and told them James Junior is my brother."

"I didn't tell them, they told me."

"So what? They sure backed down when they found out."

Sterling looked at me like he could punch me in the eye. "Shut up," he said, "you're an idiot and there's no hope for you so just shut up."

He was mad at me again and I could have cried out loud not knowing what I had said this time to make him turn on me like that.

We went home and I huddled up to the stingy warmth of the radiator in the dining room wondering why people were so eager to believe that James Junior killed that white man. The lawyer Robert got for him and Vallie told Daddy the police hadn't even filed any charges yet but was holding them all on suspicion.

At first Daddy said he would get the public defender to do for Junior, but Mother said that every time the public defender handled Pee Wee's case, he was Mrs. Caldwell's oldest boy, that poor Pee Wee got time. Mother said maybe it would be better to get Robert's lawyer friend who was connected with the Black League for Defense. Daddy said the lawyer cost a hundred and fifty dollars to start with and we didn't have no hundred and fifty dollars.

Then Mother told Daddy her dream. "I dreamed this house fell right into the ground," she said. "I was inside here, in the dining room, and it began to crumble and cave in like it was exploding, only there was no sound. Then suddenly I was standing outside looking at the pile of bricks where this house had been, and I couldn't find nobody, not you or the kids, nobody. I knew you were all buried under the house, but I couldn't do nothing but stand there and look."

"That's this house number," Daddy said. "It's gonna play today." They loaded up on 452 but it didn't come out and the next day Daddy borrowed a hundred and fifty dollars from Jocko and got Robert's lawyer friend for James Junior.

Sukie broke into my thoughts. She was outside banging on my door and hollering for me. I got up from the radiator and let her in.

"Let's go for a walk," she said.

I put on my coat and galoshes and we went downstairs and turned up 118th Street. We stopped when we saw China Doll standing in her doorway. Her thick black hair was pushed up under a tam, and her coat was open and you could see her breasts trying to jump out of her dress, it was cut that low down. One of her eyes was swollen and there were three red bruises on her cheek, like something sharp had scratched her there. Alfred again, I thought. Denise, cocoa-brown and pretty, another whore who lived in that building, was standing on the stoop with China.

"Hello China. Hello Denise."

"Hello girls," Denise said, turning toward the door. "I'm going on upstairs," she told China, and left.

"You girls coming to visit me, or just passing through?" China Doll asked.

"Coming to visit you," I said quickly. Sukie was so evil she might have told her the truth, that we were just roaming around.

China moved over and we leaned up against the stoop with her. We never went inside her house but would hang around her stoop until we saw either my Daddy or her pimp coming, then we'd leave in a hurry.

China Doll was nice. She never asked us to run any errands for her and often gave us a dime if she had it. If she didn't, she would apologize and promise to double up the next time she saw us, which she did. Once she told us that hustling was just a job to her, better than breaking her back like her mother did for pennies a day. She said ofays were gonna get you one way or the other so you might as well make them pay for it and try to give them a dose of clap in the bargain. Then she excused herself for talking like that in front of us. Later I asked Sukie what a dose of clap was.

"You jivin' or you really that ignorant?" Sukie asked. She wouldn't tell me, but I really don't think she knew either.

A white man walked by slowly, his eyes popping out of his head as he looked at China's bouncing bosom. Better get a good look now, peckerwood, I thought, and be out of Harlem before sundown.

Like most grownups, China was always telling us that we were gonna have a better break than she had and we'd better get ready for it. "You better go on and get your schooling," she was telling Sukie now. Sukie played hooky almost as much as James Junior did. All you gotta do is lay up there and learn that stuff and—"

Sukie cut her off. "Like you did?" she asked. "I hear the truant officer had to hunt you up so often you two got to be real tight."

"Don't get sassy with me," China said, but she wasn't mad 'cause she took a fifty-cent piece from between her breasts and handed it to her sister. The white man who had passed by before was strolling back. "Split this with Francie," China said, "and you all better leave now so I can get back to work."

"You're goddamn right," a deep baritone voice said behind us, and I looked up into the tough face of China's pimp, Alfred. The sun bounced off a big diamond he wore on his pinky, making rainbow sparks, and I wondered if that ring had put the scratches on China Doll's face.

"Don't cuss in front of these girls, Alfred," China Doll said mildly.

"Why not? They know more cuss words than I do."

"I don't care," China was stubborn. "It ain't nice to cuss in front of children."

"Children!" Alfred's laughter was booming. "How old are you Sukie?"

"Going on fourteen."

"Old enough to turn a trick. How old was you, China when—"

"Shut up," China Doll yelled in a sudden rage, "and take your evil eye off my sister. If you ever lay one stinking finger on her, you bastard, I swear I'll kill you."

"Stop hollering at me, you bitch. Whose talking about touching a hair on her head?"

"It ain't the hair on her head I'm worried about."

Muttering to himself that she was a crazy whore and who was cursing now in front of the children, Alfred went back inside.

"You all go on home now," China said, avoiding our eyes.

We walked on down the block. I wondered why China put up with Alfred calling her a whore when it was her money which put that diamond on his finger. "I bet China Doll could make out just as well without that old pimp," I said to Sukie. "Who needs him?"

"She does, you stupid ass."

"How come you callin' me stupid?"

Suddenly Sukie was hollering at me, her moriney face redder than an apple. "Shut up, stupid. Shut up." Then she turned and looked back at China's stoop and yelled: "And both of you go and screw yourselves."

It was the second time today somebody had called me

out of my name—first Sterling and now Sukie—and I was getting sick of it. But I didn't say anything as I followed Sukie down the street wondering what had set her off and hoping she would cool down and not forget to change that fifty cents and give me my quarter, but if she did forget I certainly wasn't gonna remind her, seeing as how she was suddenly in such a nasty mood.

And to top it all off there was Daddy waiting for us down the block. "What you girls doing on this street?"

"We're only passing through, Daddy."

"I'm gonna pass through your hide with my razor strop if I catch you on this block again. And that goes for you, too, Sukie."

"Yes, Mr. Coffin."

We ran down the rest of the block to impress Daddy, knowing all the while he was never gonna whip us.

"FRANCIE. It's seven thirty. Get up."

"Yes, Mother."

I snuggled deeper down under the big black coat that was my covering. Seemed like I had just gotten the chill out of my bones and here it was time to get up again. My breath was nice and warm and I blew it out slowly between my breasts, letting the warmth spread all over me. I don't know where we got all the old raggedy men's coats we used for blankets but I had two of them. They were more heavy than warm and had a split down the back so my feet were always sticking out, my long, long feet, always cold. I doubled myself up in a ball and finally got my feet tucked under the tail end of a coat.

"Francie. You up yet?"

"Yes, Mother."

I stuck my head under the pillow and shut my eyes

tightly. I was drifting on a warm cloud toward the sun. I could feel its rays on my arms, my back, uncurling my toes. How delicious to be unfrozen at last.

Was Junior warm enough in jail? It was gray there, with no sun. Cold and damp. And they had gray thin blankets and ate a gluey mess out of gray tin plates. Everybody knew that, we'd seen it in enough movies. Lord! Was Junior warm enough in that jail?

I tried to push the thought of him away and enjoy my sleepy warmth, but it was too late. He had come, uncalled for, like he often did during the day when I'd be playing jacks with Maude or reading or something, and then it would be spoilt and I'd have to give up whatever I was doing and brood about Junior.

They beat you in jail. Everybody knew it. We'd seen that in enough movies, too. The cops always knew who did it but the prisoner wouldn't talk so they took him down to the basement and threw him in this chair and turned those hot bright lights on him. They stood around him in a circle, shouting, while he sweated and screamed his innocence. Then they brought out the rubber hose and . . .

No. They wouldn't do that to Junior. Anybody could look at his sweet face and see he couldn't kill nobody. But was he warm? Was Junior warm in jail?

The pillow was yanked off my head and the cold morning rushed in.

"Get up from there, Francie. I'm not going to call you again."

"Yes, Mother."

I jumped up, wincing as my feet hit the icy floor and a draft of air from a crack in the window set me to shivering. Dragging my clothes behind me I ran into the bathroom and threw some ice water from the hot-water tap in my gen-

eral direction, then stumbled to the radiator in the dining
room and felt it. Barely warm. If we wasn't the janitor I
would of banged on the pipe with my shoe.

I was bending down putting on my stockings when I saw
it—two huge black eyes staring up at me from the hole in the
floor near the radiator. Two eyes and nothing more. I became quite still, my eyes locked with those in the floor-
board. Saliva flooded my mouth and my heart beat so fast I
could feel it roaring in my head. I was too afraid to even
cry out. And then around the eyes I saw the faint outline of a
huge furry head. Panic boiled up inside of me and I knew
that if I moved, even dared to breathe hard, I would start
screaming and never stop.

Then Sterling was there in his long drawers peering down
into the hole with me. "It's only a cat, Francie," he said quietly, sensing I was out of my mind with fear. "It's only a
damn cat."

Now I could see the rest of the furry head, a cat's nose
and whiskers around the thin line of its mouth.

"Scat." Sterling stamped on the hole three times. "Get
out of here." When he moved his foot the eyes were gone.

Mother came out of the kitchen. "What's the matter?"

"There was a cat in the hole," Sterling said. "Looked like
Max the Baker's cat. Must have climbed up here through
the walls somehow."

"Lord, what next?" Mother said. "When you come home
from school, Sterling, tack a piece of cardboard over that
hole. Looks like that stingy landlord ain't never gonna fix it.
Francie, you ever gonna get dressed this morning? You
gonna be late for school again."

I dragged my eyes away from the hole. It was only a cat,
I kept telling myself, but the panic wouldn't die down. Even
when I finally got dressed and was in the kitchen eating my

oatmeal, I couldn't stop shivering and it wasn't from the cold. I kept remembering that feeling of being on the edge of exploding into a thousand pieces, like Humpty-Dumpty, and all the King's horses and all the King's men couldn't put Humpty-Dumpty together again.

ONE afternoon I went with Daddy to the barber shop on Lenox Avenue to pay off a hit from yesterday because the barber shop had closed early the night before when Daddy got the money. Daddy wasn't staying out most of the night playing poker like he used to but coming home early now, and if James Junior hadn't been cooped up down there in that jail, things would've been nice.

Daddy knew just about everybody and we stopped and talked to people on the way.

"Hello, Francie, hello, Mr. Coffin. How's the missus?"

"She's fine, Mr. Lipschwitz. And your wife?"

"Great, great." It was the Jewish plumber. "Mr. Coffin, you know how my wife likes to buy new furniture."

Indeed we did, I thought, most of our furniture upstairs and the piano was a result of his wife's love for new things.

"Our old furniture is gorgeous yet," Mr. Lipschwitz said. "A fortune it cost me, but already the missus got to buy a new couch to match a picture frame. Can you imagine? So if you want our old couch, Mr. Coffin, which is like new, believe me, I would—"

Daddy interrupted him. "I sure appreciate that, Mr. Lipschwitz, but the couch we have is in excellent condition. But thanks just the same."

Daddy must be sick, I thought. *Our* old couch in excellent condition? The springs were poking up so bad that if you weren't careful when you sat down you could get stabbed to death. We walked on.

Mr. Rathbone and his pretty daughter, Rachel, were entering the candy store, her rosy cheeks peeking out over the collar of her fur coat.

"Hello, Mr. Rathbone, hello, Rachel."

"Ah, Mr. Coffin, nasty day we got already, ain't it?"

We turned the corner of Fifth Avenue.

"Mr. Coffin. You just the man I was hopin' to see."

"Hello, Slim Jim. What can I do for you?"

"What you like for the middle figure, Mr. Coffin?"

"My chart gives a four and my chart been hittin' pretty good lately."

"You really think it gonna be a four?"

"Yeah," Daddy laughed. "I feel it in my left hind leg."

"Well, I got one last dollar and two minutes to get on down to the corner and play it on a four."

"How do, Mr. Coffin."

"Good evening, Mrs. Petrie." Daddy tipped his hat. "How are you and the little one?"

Mrs. Petrie smiled and patted her stomach. She looked like that little one was gonna drop between her legs at any moment. "Mr. Coffin, if you get a minute tomorrow could you come by and show us how to make a jumper? Our electricity was shut off this morning."

"I'll be happy to, Mrs. Petrie. I'll come about five, before it gets dark." They both laughed.

"Hello, Mrs. Taylor," Daddy said. "How's your rheumatism?"

"Tolerable, Mr. Coffin, just tolerable."

We went inside the barber shop. Only two other men were there besides Mr. Robinson, the owner, and they were both barbers, too. One of them was cutting the other's hair.

"Hello, Francie," Mr. Robinson said. He was bald, head as clean as a baby's behind, and he seemed anxious for everybody to follow his lead. "When you gonna let me give you a boyish bob?" he asked me.

"I'm trying to get it to grow, Mr. Robinson, and you always want to cut it off." We smiled at each other.

"That's my business, Francie. That's my business."

Daddy handed Mr. Robinson his money and he returned five dollars of it to Daddy as a tip. "Here comes Larry," Mr. Robinson said, as Daddy was thanking him, "coming to get his."

The door opened and a young white cop entered. "And how is everybody this evening?" he smiled.

In answer, Mr. Robinson held out a bill which the cop pocketed, still smiling, and walked out.

"It ain't fair for them to be collecting twice," Daddy said. "The bankers pay them off."

"I made the mistake of opening my big mouth and talking to him just because he seemed so nice and friendly," Mr. Robinson said. "He was always asking me what number I liked and when he found out it played yesterday he came in saying how he knew I was gonna remember him. The bastard. Excuse me, Francie. But who you gonna complain to?"

"Nobody," Daddy said. "When you got a district attorney as crooked as Dodge, what can you expect from the rest of them? They're all gangsters except Mayor La Guardia and give him enough time and he'll catch on to how it's done."

"Yeah," Mr. Robinson said. "He's a peckerwood like the rest of them. I kinda like the Little Flower though and hope he stays clean. Lord knows we need one honest man down there with them bunch of crooks. How's your boy, Mr. Coffin? They still got him, huh?"

Mr. Robinson's voice had changed, like most everybody's

did when they asked about James Junior, like they was talkin' about somebody already dead.

"Yeah," Daddy answered. "They still holding all of them." He shook his head slowly. "I still can't believe it's happened, though I been warning that boy and warning him. Keep away from that gang. Stay in school and get you an education. But what you gonna do these days with these hardheaded children? I done beat him till I got sick."

"Well, Mr. Coffin, everybody knows you're a good family man, and you can only raise your kids to the best of your ability and that's all you can do. And Junior was such a nice boy, too, well mannered and friendly. No, he really wasn't the mugging type, but that friend of his. What's his name? That Sonny. I don't like to talk about other people's children but he'd mug a dead man. And he wasn't even arrested, was he?"

"No," Daddy said. "He wasn't in the cellar when the cops raided it." He spoke quietly like he'd been doing ever since Junior was arrested. I thought he would have yelled and cursed something awful when he found out about it, but he didn't. Never raised his voice, talked quiet like he was doing now, as if all his anger had gone now that Junior had finally gotten into trouble.

"I'm a grown man," Daddy said. "I play a little poker and the numbers because I can't see the difference between betting at the races or in Harlem. Either gambling's a crime or it ain't. But I've never hit a man in the head, black or white, and robbed him of his money."

"Peckerwood ain't had no business in Harlem in the middle of the night nohow," Mr. Robinson muttered. "Heard he'd been to see that whore, Denise. Excuse me, Francie."

"That's all right, Mr. Robinson," I said.

"You been down to see him yet, Mr. Coffin?"

"Four or five times. Went down there the night they arrested him and I had to threaten to tear that place apart brick by brick before they'd finally let me in, but they did. Junior told me he didn't do it and I believe him. He may be hardheaded but my boy ain't nobody's liar."

"A nice boy Junior was," Mr. Robinson said, "and polite. Always spoke nice and polite to everybody."

"Well, I gotta be getting on back home, Mr. Robinson," Daddy said. "Thanks for the fiver. You get another good dream like that let me know so I can put something on it myself."

"I'll do just that," Mr. Robinson said. "Nice seein' you again, too, Francie, and soon's you want that haircut you let me know."

We walked back down to Fifth Avenue, me slipping and sliding on the icy streets and holding on to Daddy's hand. The snow was banked up in the gutters in raggedy piles, taller than me, and it was filthy with dog pee and garbage just like I'd known it would be. But I hardly noticed it or the cold. I was still thinking about Junior. The Tombs. That's where he was. That sounded like he was already dead, too, but he wasn't, and I wished people would stop talking about him like he was gone forever.

When we got back to Fifth Avenue three of the skinniest black people I'd ever seen was standing in front of Max the Baker's window looking at the rolls inside. The woman was no bigger than a minute and the two men beside her not much larger. We watched them for a moment and it didn't take a magician to see that they were hungry. Then they turned and walked down the avenue.

Slim Jim passed by and said: "You were right, Mr. Coffin. It's a four in the middle. Thanks for the tip. I got it for a dollar."

"Me, too," Daddy said. He rushed into the bakery and came out a few seconds later with a bagful of rolls. Running down the street he caught up with the three people just as they were crossing 117th Street.

Daddy brought them back to the stoop with him, each one of them devouring one of Max's cinnamon buns. "This here is my little girl, Francie," Daddy said, introducing me to Mrs. Snipes, her husband, Tom, and her brother, Joshua. "They're gonna sleep downstairs in the basement tonight. Run upstairs and ask your mother if we got an extra blanket they can use."

I opened my mouth to say we didn't have any extra blankets and was sleeping under old coats ourselves, but I kept quiet and went on upstairs and did like I was told.

"We ain't got no extra blankets," Mother said. "What your father think? If we had any extra blankets we'd be using them ourselves."

The next morning was Saturday and I went down to the basement to visit Lilah. That was her name, and if she hadn't been so skinny and puny looking she might have been pretty with her brown-skin self.

We sat on two old stained mattresses, with the stuffing coming out, piled in front of the furnace. That's where they had slept, with all those rats running loose. But I guess even with the rats, sleeping in front of the furnace was better than being out in the cold.

Lilah said they were from Virginia, sharecroppers, but things had been so poorly down there that after her baby died they decided to come north where things might be better. But now, having no home at all, they were sorry they had ever left the south.

"You had a baby?" I asked.

She nodded. "A little girl. She died when she was a week old." She touched her flat chest. "I didn't have no milk."

Her husband and brother had gone out early that morning to try and hustle up a day's work.

"They ain't gonna find nothing," Lilah said, "but they scared to break the habit of looking, like that might jinx them or something."

Daddy brought home some greens and salt pork around midday and Mother cooked them and made some corn bread and gave me some to take down to the basement.

Tom and Joshua were quiet and soft-spoken. They smiled at me when I handed them the food and said: "Thank you, ma'am." It was the first time anybody had ever called me ma'am and it made me feel funny and grown-up.

I took them down one meal a day after that, whatever we had. Mother got so hard up that she had to fall back on that gold-can jive. She didn't even have no tomatoes to doctor it up with and we was eating it warmed up straight from the can.

I had told Mother, laughing all the while, how Daddy had refused Mr. Lipschwitz's couch, saying ours was in excellent condition. Now I was sorry I had opened my big mouth 'cause Mr. Lipschwitz's couch appeared in our living room a few days later and Mother and Sterling hauled our old wreck down to the basement.

Daddy had a fit when he saw the new couch and stormed into the kitchen to find Mother. "I told that old Jew we didn't want his hand-me-down furniture," he said.

"How come you told him that when our old couch was looking so bad?" Mother asked.

"Because I didn't want it, woman. Can't you understand plain English?"

"All the insides was hanging out of our couch and the living room looked so tacky I was ashamed to have anybody stop by. Mr. Lipschwitz always gives us his old furniture. How come you—"

"Because I just didn't want it."

Mother sighed. "I don't know how Francie been sleeping on that old couch with those springs punching her in her bones all these months."

The new sofa did sleep much better than the old one and the bugs hadn't gotten into the springs yet but I knew they was coming and I felt real bad now like me and Mother had ganged up on Daddy.

Daddy didn't say another word to Mother, just marched into the front room and sat down on the piano stool, staring at the piano keys.

"You gonna play, Daddy?" I rubbed my head against his shoulder.

He patted me absent-minded, and then pushed me gently away, still staring at those keys like they would unlock the door to somewhere. He stayed like that for about an hour, then he got up and went out and didn't come back all night.

We were still off relief, and what with Daddy's commissions all going to Jocko to pay for Junior's lawyer, and feeding the people in the basement, we were even running out of the gold-can jive which I swear *was* horsemeat, it was that stringy and strong.

About a week later me and Mother met Sonny's grandmother in the street. She said she had just come from the relief office and had gotten a clothing allowance for Sonny.

"Lord, how did you manage that?" Mother asked.

"I put some soap in my mouth," Mrs. Taylor said, "and when they got to acting like they wasn't gonna give me anything I just started foaming at the mouth like a mad dog."

Mother smiled. "We ain't on relief at all. We been cut off for months."

"Mrs. Coffin, don't let them folks down there mess with you. President Roosevelt said that money was to keep poor folks from starving and God knows he had to be talking about us. Just go on down there and act bad and they'll put you back on relief just to get rid of you."

Mother said she would do it but the next day when she kept me out of school and hauled me down to the relief office with her, I knew she wasn't about to pitch no fit.

The relief place was across the street from Mt. Morris Park and all we did was sit around that office all day long, seeing one supervisor then waiting years to see the supervisor's supervisor. What a system. We had been there since nine o'clock and had seen four people and it was almost three now.

I was standing next to Mother who was sitting at the desk of our fifth interviewer. This one, whose bumpy, thin face was screwed into a frown like she was smelling pee all day long, was the head flunky, I hoped. She preached at Mother like she was a thief for trying to get even so all our checks wouldn't have to go to Mr. Burnett. We had sinned. She made that clear.

"Even if your husband didn't report his janitor's job, Mrs. Coffin, you should have done so," she said. "After all, it's a mother's duty to be truthful and God-fearing and set an example for her children. Do you know you violated a section of the emergency relief code?"

Mother nodded slowly, accepting her guilt. She didn't report that she, too, was working, bootlegging domestic work, and if she was gonna rat on anybody it should be on herself.

She spoke softly, agreeing with everything the supervisor said. She had been wrong not to report her husband's job and she would never do that again the Lord knew but her children were hungry so please forgive us our sins this one time and give us our daily bread and another supply of dried prunes and butter and that gold-can shit.

I sat there looking like a ragpicker in my scuffed sneakers and patched skirt, one of Mother's hungry children, wide-eyed and innocent.

Go fuck yourself, I said silently to the pimply face humbling my mother. The supervisor suddenly looked like Madame Queen, all of them did, although they were white. I was too mad to cry. I would have yelled out loud or hit the woman were it not for the look on my mother's face. Where had I seen that look before? At whose funeral?

Never beg nobody for nothing.

Then suddenly I knew. Mother was beating herself with the thick end of the razor strop.

We walked out of the relief office fast, glad to get away from that place. Mother was blinking and sniffing and I looked at her, scared. Was that a tear in the corner of her eye? Everybody had a right to cry when they got a whipping. Everybody. I grabbed hold of her hand as we was crossing the street and held on to it hard. She squeezed it lightly, looking down at me. Her eyes were dry. Holding on to each other we stumbled on home.

We got back on relief too late to help our basement friends. They left before we even got our first check, saying they were going to try and hitchhike back to Virginia where at least they wouldn't freeze to death while starving.

I hated to see them go. If we had been able to feed them more often and with something else besides that damned horsemeat, maybe they would have stayed up here. I thought about James Junior and Vallie cooped up in jail and China Doll and Sukie and everybody's mother and mine begging our way back on relief. I even thought about old mannish Saralee. We were all mixed up in something together, us colored up here in the north, something I couldn't quite figure out. But it was better up here than down south. That's what I'd always heard people say, that folks down in Bip were just dying for a chance to come north to the promised land. This *was* the promised land, wasn't it?

Mother never did tell Daddy how we got back on relief and he never did ask her. Had he known, he would have disowned us both.

NINE

A MONTH after they was arrested James Junior and three other boys were let loose. It was a nice Christmas present but nobody could get too hysterical over it 'cause Vallie and the Washington boys were still in jail. They had confessed to mugging that white man to death and were gonna be tried for murder. They swore that the others had nothing to do with it and weren't even present.

While they were about it they also confessed to three other muggings and holding up two pawnshops. Before that, though, Sonny had gone downtown all by himself and told them that James Junior had been in the Jewel Theatre with him when that man got killed and when they left the movie Junior had gone to the gang's hangout while Sonny went home. Everybody said that was a real brave thing for Sonny to do since they could have snatched his butt, too, while he was down there, him being an Ebony Earl and all.

Daddy went to get James Junior and bring him home. Mother cried and hugged him and cried some more. It was the first time I had ever seen her cry. Sterling shook James Junior's hand, pumping it up and down and grinning like a fool, then they flung each other's hands away and hugged. James Junior kissed me all over my face. We were laughing and grabbing hold of Junior like we couldn't get enough of him.

Then we all sat down to dinner together like we hadn't done in a long time. Mother must have borrowed something from everybody in the neighborhood, 'cause we had string beans with ham hocks and potatoes, pickled beets, corn bread, and Junior's favorite for dessert, apple dumplings.

While me and Mother did the dishes, Junior and Sterling helped Daddy practice for a party he was going to that night. Then we was all in the front room hanging around the piano and laughing at nothing like we was crazy.

"Oh, Lord," Mother said suddenly, flinging her hand up over her mouth, "we over here laughing out loud and forgot all about poor Mrs. Caldwell."

"Yeah," Junior said, his smile fading, "I gotta see her. Every time she goes to visit Vallie she cries so hard that he don't want her to come down there no more. He told me to tell her that. That he loves her but he don't want her to make herself sick like she been doin' coming down there and getting upset."

Even though Robert hadn't wanted Mrs. Caldwell to go down to the jail, like Daddy wouldn't let Mother go, Mrs. Caldwell went anyhow, saying a boy in trouble had to have at least one parent come to see him and the devil himself wasn't gonna keep her home.

"Well, let's go over the roof and see her now," Daddy said. "I've got to leave soon for my party."

We trooped over the roof and it was just like a funeral over there, the whole family sitting around very quiet not discussing the news.

Mrs. Caldwell was rocking Elizabeth's baby in her lap.

Back and forth the rocker squeaked, the only sound in the room. It was worse than a wake. Mr. Caldwell's wake, in fact, had been nice, all the neighbors bringing in food and wine. The only time it was real sad was at the cemetery when Mrs. Caldwell started wailing. But this was worse 'cause there was no eating and drinking and no funeral coming and no Vallie to put away decently in the ground.

The next day the boys' pictures were in the *Times,* the three of them lookin' thin and scared. The Washington boys had been up to our house that time Daddy hit the number and we had a party. I read now that Luke was the ringleader of the gang. The paper said:

"Three undersized Negro schoolboys confessed to having killed Lester Farley of 2842 Broadway, a month ago, in a Harlem hallway at 14 W. 118th St. The youthful trio admitted to having terrorized white men in their community for at least a year and confessed to three other holdups.

"The oldest boy, Luke Washington, 18, is regarded as the brains of the gang. He told how he and his brother, Calvin, 17, and Vallejo Caldwell, 16, 'mugged' Farley and robbed him of twenty dollars. 'Mugging' is a method by which one grips a victim's neck while an accomplice goes through his pockets.

"The dead man was a salesman in a shoe store on 116th Street, was married and had two daughters, 7 and 13. All three defendants are members of a notorious street gang, the Ebony Earls."

That was the first time I knew that the dead man had two daughters and I wondered why he had been roamin' around on Harlem rooftops and in the movies when he had such a nice family at home. The papers didn't say what he was doing on 118th Street when he was killed, but everybody knew he'd been visiting Denise, the prostitute.

When I saw Sonny in the street a few days later, I marched right up to him, but after mumbling "hello" I got tongue-tied and stood there forever before I finally got out what I wanted to say.

"I wanna thank you, Sonny, for doing what you did for James Junior."

Sonny looked across the street. "Well, Junior's my buddy, you know. We's tight."

"It was still a brave thing to do. Daddy said you could have been arrested, too, when you went down there."

"Aw, Francie, it wasn't nothin'." He looked down at his shoes with sudden interest, like he just noticed he was wearing them.

I wanted to kiss his cheek like the girls do in the movies when they want to tell a guy they'd like to be just friends, but I didn't know how to do it, so I mumbled again how brave he was and backed away.

Later that week I heard Daddy and Robert talking through the air shaft, both of them bundled up in their winter coats 'cause it was freezin' outside. Mother was at work and I was dusting up in the front room.

"They beat Vallie and the Washington brothers to make them confess," Robert said.

"Yeah, I know," Daddy said, "James Junior told me. Said he didn't want to mention it in front of the women but he told me later."

"They beat Junior, too?"

"Roughed him up a little bit, but nothing like the workout they gave the others. Jesus Christ, if I could just get my hands around the neck of that cop that hit my boy."

"Bastards," Robert said. "They got you in jail where you can't run and still they have to whip you. Know what they did to a friend of mine in Chicago? Put this electric wire on his balls and when that shock hit him he said he woulda confessed to killin' Jesus Christ if they had asked him to."

"You don' think . . ."

"No, they wouldn't do nothin' like that in New York. Not to kids anyway."

"You think they killed that man?"

Robert took his time answering, then finally said: "I think so, Mr. Coffin. I think so."

They talked a little longer but I wasn't listening. Robert had to be wrong. If James Junior couldn't kill anybody then neither could Vallejo. Sure, he might mug some old white man in a hallway but he wouldn't kill him. Why didn't they stop beating those boys down there in the Tombs long enough to discover it was an accident? I was just about to cry when a thought stopped me. I could never tell Maude and Rebecca what I had just heard. It would be too terrible on top of everything else for them to know that the cops had beaten the shit out of their brother.

Before long Daddy and Junior were staying out late again just like before. Daddy was playing poker most of the night and Junior fell right back in with the Ebony Earls like he'd never been away, beating Daddy home every night by an eyelash.

All winter long we kept up with Vallie's case in the papers. The *News* didn't mention it again after the first week but the big papers Daddy liked to read did, and I took to reading them sometimes, which would have made Daddy happy if he'd been home to see me. There wasn't much news about Negroes in the big papers and what was written was usually bad. And the colored paper, *The Amsterdam News,* mostly told about lynchings down south and niggers killing each other up north. It was kind of depressing.

I WAS in trouble at school. If I didn't get a book full of recipes for the cooking class and finish my dress for the sewing class, I was gonna flunk both those courses for the midterm. I hated cooking and always sneaked out. They gave you a thimble full of this and half an eyedropper of that and you was supposed to copy down the recipe from the blackboard and follow it and cook the crap they gave you. The only time I stayed in cooking class for the full time we made shepherd's pie. Now I wouldn't have minded learning how to cook mustard greens or pig tails, but they didn't teach us stuff like that, so I just stopped going, and naturally I didn't have no notebook full of recipes.

Sewing was just as bad. You was supposed to make a dress by hand by midterm and get graded on it. The class had to do everything together, sew up the seams, start on the sleeves, hemstitch. I used to get through quicker than anybody else and my teacher, Mrs. Abowitz, would make me wait for the rest of the class before I could go to the next step. She did say that if I worked my backstitch more neatly I wouldn't get through so fast, but I got tired waiting around so I took to cutting sewing, too. When I ditched classes like that I would go into the toilet and sit there and read my library book or some smutty stories, if I had any.

That's what I was doing now while pondering the trouble I was in, sitting on the toilet seat reading some smutty comic books. I had three of them, Mutt and Jeff screwing two girls at the same time, Jiggs doing it to Maggie, and Little Orphan Annie almost swallowed up under Daddy Warbucks. The books were in color just like the Sunday comics but was more exciting.

Then I got the idea where I could get my recipes from. Most of my friends were as bad off as me, they might have some of the recipes but not all, but Joan, the only white girl in my class, she always went to cooking.

I felt sorry for Joan because she didn't have any friends. That was her fault mostly 'cause she stuck to herself all the time and was very snotty. But I guess it wasn't any fun to still be living on 119th Street after all the other white folks had moved away and you had to go to school with niggers and Puerto Ricans. Me and Maude had tried to make friends with her, but said to hell with it when she stuck her freckled nose up in the air and ignored us. But in algebra today when we were trading our smutty books, I noticed Joan looking kinda wistfully at my collection.

I rushed back to my homeroom and cornered her just as class was being dismissed. "Hi, Joan," I said, like I hadn't been seeing her all day. "How you been?"

She nodded her head slowly, "Fine, thank you."

"I was wondering, Joan, if maybe you'd like to borrow my comic books this afternoon."

"You mean the . . ."

"Yeah, those are the ones I mean."

"Well, gee, Francie, that would be nice of you." She sort of half smiled at me.

"And in the meantime, can I borrow your recipe book? There's one or two I missed."

Her half smile was dying.

"I just wanna copy a few recipes, Joan. That ain't gonna hurt nobody."

"Well, I don't know . . ."

"And anytime I get any more of these dirty books I'll save them for you."

"You will?"

"Honest."

"Well, okay, but I don't have my notebook with me."

"I'll stop by your house and pick it up on my way home and give it back to you in the morning. You live on 119th Street, don't you? What's the address?"

"One twenty-two."

"Okay, I'll be there in a few minutes and bring the books with me," and before she could change her mind I turned away.

I gave Joan five minutes' head start, then I went by her house. She lived with her mother in a three-story brownstone, on the street level, and they had a separate entrance on the side. I went to the door which had an iron gate in front of it and rang the bell. Joan's white face peaked around a curtain, then she cracked the door open.

"Just a minute," she said, "I'll get my cookbook."

She was gone for about five minutes and I was just about to ring the bell again when she came back, and unchaining the iron gate, came outside.

"What took you so long?"

"My mother was asking me who you were."

"Oh."

She handed me the book and I gave her the smutty stories. She turned, and the iron gate clanged shut behind her. I went home, feeling a little evil 'cause she had made me wait outside instead of inviting me in and introducing me to her mother.

At home as I copied the recipes, I thought, screw Joan, but she did have a nice, neat handwriting.

I turned in my cookbook the next day. Mrs. McCarthy, the teacher, looked at me like I was a stranger, which I almost was, but there were so many kids in her class that she didn't know them all anyway so she couldn't be sure whether I was there most of the time or not. She went through the notebook very suspiciously, I thought, but I smiled sweetly at her when she looked up at me, and she mumbled, "Very good," and gave me A minus.

I don't think I quite fooled Mrs. Abowitz, my sewing teacher. Maude's dress was a mess and fitted her like a sack, but at least it was done and I had only one side of mine together and couldn't possibly finish it now. So after Maude got graded on her dress, I talked her into letting me borrow it.

"I don't remember seeing you in class very often, Francie," Mrs. Abowitz said, as she peered at Maude's sloppy seams through her double-lens glasses.

"I been here," I mumbled.

"If you would take more time with your backstitch, Francie, you might make a good seamstress one day. That's a very good living, you know."

"I don't think I'd like it, Mrs. Abowitz. I want to be a secretary when I grow up."

"Well, Francie, we have to be practical. There aren't very many jobs for Negroes in that field. And while you're going to school you should learn those things which will stand you in good stead when you have to work."

"I like shorthand and typing, Mrs. Abowitz," I said, suddenly stubborn, "and I'm gonna be a secretary."

She sighed. "I don't know why they teach courses like that to frustrate you people."

I'm almost sure Mrs. Abowitz knew that dress wasn't mine, but for some reason, while she had only given Maude a C on it, she gave me a B plus.

To celebrate passing my midterms, I talked Mother into giving me some money to buy some new shoes and to let me go and get them by myself. Well, Mother did ask Rebecca to go with me and make sure I got a good buy, but it was practically like shopping by myself, which was good, 'cause

I usually had a terrible time with Mother. She was always trying to put some baby-looking flat shoes on my big feet. Now I was gonna buy a pair with a little heel.

First, though, me and Becky went to Kress's on 125th Street to mosey around. It was always fun going into the Five and Ten even if you didn't have the money to buy anything with. We looked at the pretty flowers for a dime, with a comb in them to stick in your hair, and the silk stockings for thirty-nine cents, which cost ten cents less under the Bridge. Then we casually walked over to the cookie counter and when the salesgirl turned to ring up a sale we both swiped a chocolate cookie and hurried outside.

We ate it while walking the half block to the shoe store and looked at the shoes in the window. "That's the kind I want," I told Becky, pointing to a black patent leather with a nice, neat heel.

We went inside the crowded store and found a seat. For some reason Miles Shoe Store and National's, too, right next door, were always crowded.

"These shoes ain't nothing but cardboard," a lady next to us said. "If they last a month they'll be doing good."

"So," the white salesman replied, "for a dollar ninety-eight you want leather?"

Me and Becky grinned. "I want to see number seven oh four," I told the salesman. I would play that number tomorrow. "Size seven."

The salesman got the shoe and crammed my right foot into it.

"That shoe's too tight for you," Becky said, as I stood up and limped to the mirror.

"No, it's not," I said quickly. If it killed me I wasn't gonna get a bigger size. My foot was larger than everybody else's already.

"Your mother told me to see that you got the right size," Becky said, acting grown-up and tough. She turned to the salesman. "You got this a half size larger?"

"I tell you, Becky, it fits just fine." The shoes were shiny and pretty with a ribbon bow and a round toe which was pinching me but they were gonna stretch for christsakes.

"They gonna stretch and be too big," I told the salesman when he fitted me with the larger size.

"Stand up," he said.

I got up and walked to the mirror. These were more comfortable, but seven and a halfs! When was my feet gonna stop growing?

"They feel better?" Becky asked.

"They're too big."

"We'll take them," Becky said, sounding just like my mother.

I opened my mouth to protest but a lady ran screaming into the store and I shut up to listen to her.

"They killed him. They drug the poor child down to the basement and shot him dead."

"What you talking about, lady?" somebody asked, as a crowd gathered around her. "Who killed who?"

"The police. Shot a little colored boy at Kress's. Said he was stealing a pocket knife and they took him down to the basement to make him confess and they killed him. Over a little old knife."

A low rumble started in the store. We paid for the shoes and went outside where the news was spreading all up and down 125th Street.

"Did you hear about it? Little Puerto Rican kid beaten to death at the Five and Ten. Swiped some candy and the cops hit him too hard and he died. Goddamn bullies. He was only a kid, I hear, eleven or twelve."

"I never did like Woolworth's," a fat lady said to us. "None of these stores hire colored, but the help at Woolworth's are the hinctiest, and now they done gone and killed that child."

"It happened at Kress's," I told the lady. "Least that's what somebody told us. And me and my friend Becky was just in Kress's not more than half an hour ago. They was probably beating that boy while we . . ." My voice trailed off. I looked at Becky and she nodded. She understood what I had started to say—while we was in there swiping cookies. Lord, it coulda been us the cops got, for sure as the devil had a tail we swiped cookies every time we went to the Five and Ten. It could have been us, dead now in the basement of Kress's. Or was it Woolworth's?

We walked home, listening to the outraged protests of the people. Yeah, it was a shame. God knew it was a lowdown, dirty shame.

When Mother came home that night I rushed to tell her the news.

"Mother, me and Becky was in Kress's and . . ."

"Did you get your shoes?"

"Yes, Mother, but let me tell you . . ."

"Try them on for me. I want to make sure they're the right size."

"They fit okay, Mother. In fact, they're too big. Becky and me were . . ."

"Let me see the shoes, Francie."

I got the shoes and wiggled into them.

"Yeah, they're a good fit. Francie, please try not to kick these out so fast. Lord, but you're hard on shoes. You just had a new pair two months ago."

"Well, it's not my fault," I said, getting mad. "They ain't nothing but cardboard, that's why I kick them out so fast, and I'm trying to tell you something important and all you can think about is these old shoes."

"Who you talkin' to in that tone of voice, Francie Coffin? If you don't like them cardboard shoes then get some money and buy your own. And they would last longer if you'd pull them off after school like I keep tellin' you to do, and wear your sneakers.

"I'm sorry, Mother, I didn't mean . . ."

"What is it you trying to tell me?"

It was spoiled now. I was grateful for the shoes but somehow, how did it happen, it was all spoiled now, the excitement of telling Mother how me and Becky had been in Kress's at the time that boy got killed.

"They beat a little boy, or shot him, for stealing a knife or some candy at Kress's. Or maybe it was Woolworth's. Anyhow, it happened on 125th Street and the boy is dead."

"My God," Mother said. "What next, what next?"

What next was a riot, and I slept right through it like a dumbbell.

"They tore up 125th Street last night," Maude told me when we met the next morning to go to school.

"Who tore it up?"

"We did. Had a riot and tore 125th Street to pieces."

"Over that boy they killed," I said, excited. "Me and Becky was in Kress's right while it was happening I bet, and we didn't have enough sense to stay on 125th Street and wait for the riot. Let's go by on our way to school."

We walked up to 125th Street. It was a chilly March day, the winds whipping like sixty around the corners. The street was indeed a mess, a jungle of broken glass, overturned gar-bage cans, and all kinds of junk hauled from the stores and dumped into the street. Cops were everywhere and store-keepers were nailing up strips of wood over their broken windows. Some of those little dingy colored stores on Lenox Avenue, like the barber shop and candy store, had painted on their windows, "Owned by colored." A Jewish cleaners had written on his door, "Colored work here."

"Hey, look at that lying bastard, would you?" Maude said.

I had passed by that cleaners many a time and had never seen a Negro behind the counter. As we walked by we saw that the door had been knocked down and the inside of the store wrecked.

"He didn't fool a soul, did he?" Maude said.

As we passed Herbert's Jewelers on the corner of Seventh Avenue, I said: "I sure wished I had been here. I would have reached right inside that broken window and got me a diamond ring. I could've pawned it and been rich. But I'll tell you one thing, I'm gonna stop coming to 125th Street with Becky. Every time I do there's a riot."

We finally made it to school and was late but it didn't matter because everybody was excited and talking about the riot and we didn't have to stay after school to make it up.

The papers the next day had a full report and I read all about it. A Puerto Rican boy, 16, had stolen a knife from Kress's all right, but the cops hadn't shot him but hauled his butt off to jail. Anyhow, that started the riot and three thousand Negroes broke two hundred plate-glass windows and resisted five hundred cops. A hundred people were hurt and one was dead.

The district attorney, who Daddy said was a stooge for Dutch Schultz, said the whole thing was a Communist plot, and he was gonna throw everybody in jail.

Mayor La Guardia sent out some big signs which were put up in store windows on 125th Street and me and Sukie walked up there to see them. The sign said that most of the people in Harlem were decent, law-abiding American citizens and the riot was started by vicious individuals who spread false reports of racial discrimination.

Sukie turned and pointed a finger under my nose. "You are a law-abiding American," she said.

"No, I'm not," I answered, "I'm a vicious individual," and we fell out laughing. We read the mayor's sign again out loud, each of us reading a line and laughing. All the way home we kept punching each other and hollering: "You're vicious. No, you're decent." I laughed so hard my stomach ached and I almost didn't notice Sukie was punching me harder than I was her, but if anybody had asked me what was so funny I couldn't have told them.

The riot seemed to have driven Daddy and James Junior in from the streets 'cause they stayed close to home for the next few days. One night we were all sitting around in the front room and Daddy started reading aloud from the evening paper. He was always getting after me and Mother for reading the *Daily News,* that rag, as he called it. Said they was anti-Negro, always labeling us thugs and hoodlums and might as well come on down front and call us niggers and be done with it. But I liked the pictures in the *News,* which was easy to read, and Mother always bought it when she had two cents. She read real slow and liked the pictures, too. Those big papers Daddy liked were awfully long winded, but I was reading them often now and I told him so.

Daddy read us what Adam Clayton Powell Jr. had to say. Adam claimed colored people were mad 'cause they didn't have no jobs and was discriminated against from the cradle to the grave, and that's why they rioted. They couldn't get a job driving a bus in their own neighborhood or delivering milk in Harlem or working in the stores on

125th Street. They were also mad about the Scottsboro case and 'cause Mussolini was kicking asses in Ethiopia and the League of Nations didn't care. Adam didn't say it exactly like that but that's what he meant. He also said rents were higher in Harlem than anywhere else in the city and that these tenements were rat traps and a disgrace, and God knows that was the truth.

Daddy turned the page. "Another one is dead," he said. "Listen to this: 'Fifth Riot Victim Dies. Kenneth Hobston, 16, a Negro of 304 St. Nicholas Avenue, died in Harlem Hospital yesterday as a result of a bullet wound received during the Harlem riot. Patrolman John McDonald said that he shot into a group of boys who ran from a store they were looting. However, other witnesses stated that Hobston was merely looking at the rioting. The boy was shot in the back. The police chief has promised to investigate the matter. This is the fifth victim to die as a result of last week's rioting.' "

"What a shame," Mother said. "Sixteen years old and dead, and for what?"

"And the police chief is gonna investigate," Daddy said. "What he means is he's gonna whitewash that cop. Five people dead and four of them black. I don't know what's the matter with these niggers up north. They don't even know how to riot, just getting themselves killed smashing windows and breaking up stuff. That ain't gonna change nothing. Now we had us a riot down in Charleston when I was a boy. And we killed enough peckerwoods so that they got the message. There's never been a lynching in Charleston since then. No, by Christ. After the sheriff killed that colored man, the Negroes went down by the railroad yards and pulled up the iron ties. There was a whole army of us. I was just a young boy, but I was there. Marched right into town we did and started whipping every white head we could find with them railroad ties. Took them peckerwoods by surprise and they ain't never forgot it."

"You was in a riot, Daddy?" I asked excited. "You never told us that before."

"I did so," Daddy said. "Trouble is you all never listen to me. Yessir, them peckerwoods ain't never forgot that riot. To hell with smashing windows. You gonna smash something let it be a white man's skull. You gonna kill somebody let it count for something."

He looked hard at James Junior, letting his words soak in before he asked: "And where were you that night, you and your gang? Don't think I didn't notice that cut on your hand. You was out there looting with that gang?"

Junior avoided Daddy's eyes. "We was just wandering around."

Daddy turned to Sterling. "And where were you?"

"Who, me? I was . . . well, I was with James Junior."

Daddy shook his head. "I thought you at least had better sense, Sterling. I thought you was gonna learn how to use your brains."

I was glad Daddy didn't ask me where I was. I would have been ashamed to say I was home sleepin' right through the whole thing, although I had been in on the beginning.

Daddy turned back to Junior. "I guess being in jail once wasn't enough for you. You want to make that place your permanent home? Just keep on messing up and you will, and I swear, I ain't gonna put one foot in front of the other the next time to get you out."

"Read us some more, Daddy," I said quickly, trying to get him off of James Junior.

Daddy mumbled a bit more under his breath, then read a

short paragraph about a six-month-old baby who died in Harlem Hospital yesterday after being bitten by a rat.

The mayor named a commission to investigate the riot, and every day there were reports on what they were finding out. Like it wasn't the Communists at all that caused the riot but prejudice and hard times which gave the people the blues, just like Adam said, until they finally exploded.

Then Vallie's trial started, and that knocked all those reports, which Daddy said we niggers knew all about anyway, right out of our minds. I got *The Amsterdam News* to read about the trial 'cause although we got all the facts from the Caldwells it seemed to make it worse to read about it in the paper, too.

The headlines on all the papers that day was about Dutch Schultz. He was on trial in Albany for not paying taxes on the money he made bootlegging beer during Prohibition. A guy by the name of Dewey was trying to bust him.

Then I found the little note about Vallie and them on the back page. Their attorney had asked for a dismissal 'cause he said the boys confessed under duress. That means they whipped them. The judge said he wasn't going to allow no such thing, and ordered the jury to be picked tomorrow.

The Dutch Schultz case stayed on the front pages of the papers. There was much ado about how he ran the policy rackets and even paid off the cops, but the jury didn't find him guilty. They couldn't agree on a verdict, so old Dutch was gonna get a new trial. Everybody said he had paid off the jury like he did everybody else.

Spring came slowly, like it had to fight Old Man Winter to the grave to make him give up, and it wasn't until May that we finally took off our heavy clothes, and it was still cold and damp.

Then Vallie's trial was over and although we were all expecting it, the verdict was an awful blow. The jury stayed out for two hours. They found the three boys guilty of first-degree murder and sentenced them to die in the electric chair.

TEN

"IT took me sixteen years to raise that boy," Mrs. Caldwell said. "How could a handful of people decide in two hours that he ain't fit to live? How can they kill children who haven't grown into their manhood yet?"

Mother and I were visiting the Caldwells the afternoon the news came out. Their whole family was there.

"I tried to raise Vallejo and his brother right," Mrs. Caldwell said. "Their father did, too. He was awfully strict with them, but he loved those boys. They always knew that. And I stood between them and their father's anger many a time. Now somebody tell me what we did wrong. How could we have done it any better? I've tried and tried to figure it out. What caused my boys to take to the streets like wild animals? I prayed over them and sat up nights waiting for them to come home but none of it did any good. Now somebody tell me what me and their father did wrong. Tell me because I'm all dried up. I can't squeeze another tear out of me."

But even as she was talking the tears rolled down her cheeks, starting everybody else to crying, too.

"You all hush now," Robert said gently. "All this crying ain't gonna get us nowhere. They beat those boys to make them confess and that gives us a chance to appeal this thing. And some white people downtown are writing a petition to the governor asking him to do away with the death penalty for all minors, so we still got a chance. You all hush now, they haven't electrocuted those boys yet."

Electrocuted. The word jarred me. An electric shock had gone through me once when I was putting the jumper in. It was a quick sensation of instant pain racing through my body. Would Vallie go quickly, painlessly? Vallie, Vallie. What a strange, unnatural way for you to die.

THE next Saturday I got up early to return some library books which were overdue. Seems like I could never get them back on time, and of course I didn't have the money for the fine so I agreed to pay it off on the installment plan. I owed them thirty-four cents for these books and twelve cents from before. I promised to pay two cents each time I came in and the librarian was very nice and didn't take away my library card, and I swore one more time to get these books back before they was due.

I found Daddy and he gave me a dime for the movies, but I decided to make me some money instead by selling shopping bags under the Bridge, so I went on down there.

The Bridge was an open-air market on Park Avenue under the el for the Pennsylvania Railroad train. There were hundreds of pushcarts under the Bridge, all lined up next to each other selling everything from pickled herrings to cotton bloomers. The Bridge ran from 116th down to 110th Street, and there were stores outside on the street, too, where things were real cheap.

If you stayed down here all day you could maybe make

thirty or forty cents selling shopping bags. I went to the wholesale place and bought eight bags for a dime which I would sell for two cents apiece.

The vendors, mostly old Jews, were bundled up in two or three raggedy sweaters, the women wearing long dark skirts down to their ankles like they didn't know this was America, their faces red and raw from the wind or from the fires many of them built in trash cans behind their pushcarts. They was there all day in all kinds of weather and poor people came there in all kinds of weather, too, to save a few cents.

I don't like cold, drizzly days and I soon lost my enthusiasm for walking up one side of the market and down the other shouting: "Shopping bags, two cents. Get your shopping bag here. Bag, lady?" But I kept at it and by noon I'd sold my first eight bags and bought eight more.

Business was slow and I walked the length of the market twice before I sold another bag, then I stopped to watch a little old Jewish lady, bundled up in what looked like her grandfather's coat, it was that long, arguing with a red-faced vendor. She was accusing him of weighing his hand in along with the potatoes she was buying and he was denying it vigorously, raising his hands and his black bushy eyebrows to heaven to confirm his honesty. They was both shouting at each other and in his excitement, the man swept his arms outward and knocked four or five grapefruits from his cart to the ground. One of them rolled by my foot and I bent down, swept it into a shopping bag, and started to stroll away.

But the vendor saw me. "Stop. Thief," he shouted, and took out after me.

I started to run, looking back over my shoulder to see if he was gaining. He was huffin' and puffin' behind me, and beyond him the little old lady was scooping up the grape-fruits from the ground and putting them in her shopping bag. I stopped dead still. Just as the man reached me and was about to grab me by the shoulders, I pointed behind him and said: "You better mind your cart."

He looked back, saw what was happening, and wheeled around, hollering at the woman: "Stop, thief. Stop."

A crowd had gathered around his stand by this time and the woman disappeared behind them. When the vendor got back to his pushcart he stopped, aware that if he ran after her somebody else might help themselves to his fruit. He jumped up and down in rage, his red face getting redder, the bundle of rags he was wearing jiggling around with him. The crowd burst out laughing. The old fool should have stayed put in the first place and minded his pushcart.

I laughed, too, but suddenly, for no good reason, stopped, feeling sorry for the man, perhaps because he looked like a scarecrow with his red button nose and all those sweaters wrapped around him. I was sorry I'd picked up his stupid old grapefruit in the first place. I peeled it like an orange, and as I was eating it thought that Mother would whip my butt ragged if she knew what I'd done. Half of the grape-fruit was rotten and I threw it away in disgust. It was a long time since I had a grapefruit, so why did this one have to be rotten?

I sold the rest of my bags and crossed the street to the delicatessen 'cause I was hungry. I got a hot dog buried in sauerkraut, then bought a big sour pickle which was float-ing around in brine in a huge wooden barrel on the side-walk. The little pickles were two cents and the big ones a nickel and they were so sour they made your mouth cry.

I munched my hot dog slowly, walking down the street,

and stopped in front of a Jewish bakery and looked in the window. I had twelve cents left. I could either buy two delicious apple strudels for a dime or go back under the Bridge and sell some more shopping bags. But that grapefruit being no good after all the trouble it caused had somehow spoiled my mood for selling shopping bags, which had been none too strong to begin with. Anyway I'd been down there over four hours already so I entered the bakery and came out with the strudels. It was disgusting but I had just spent all my profit, like I usually did.

When I got back to Fifth Avenue I found out I had hit the number. Hot diggedy dog. I could hardly wait for Mother to get home to tell her the good news and when I heard her footsteps on the stairs I ran to meet her.

"Mother, guess what. Seven oh four played today and I got it for a nickel."

"A whole nickel? Francie, that's wonderful."

She came inside and plopped down at the dining-room table.

"You remember them shoes I bought at Miles, Mother? When Rebecca went with me? Well, the number on those shoes was seven oh four and I been playing it ever since. Straight."

"I wish I had me a nickel on it," Mother said. "Thirty dollars."

"We can sure use thirty dollars, can't we?" I said.

"We sure can." We smiled at each other.

"You wanna cup of tea, Mother? I'll get it for you."

I ran into the kitchen and put the pot on and made her a full cup of tea as she liked it, brimming over the top, and took it to her. Then I made one for myself. "We don't have any sugar," I said.

"See if Mrs. Caldwell's got some."

I knocked on their window and Elizabeth came to it.

"Lizzie, I hit the number for a nickel today."

"Francie. You're a lucky devil. She smiled and turned back into the room. "Ma, Francie hit the number for a nickel."

"So I already heard," Mrs. Caldwell said. "Now she can buy me a licorice stick."

"I will, Mrs. Caldwell," I hollered to her. "I will."

I held out a cup to Elizabeth. "Can we borrow some sugar?"

"Sure, if we got any." She took the cup and disappeared, returning in a moment with it filled.

"Thanks, Lizzie. I'll buy you all a whole pound tomorrow." And I would, too.

Me and Mother sat there sipping our tea and waiting for Daddy to come home with the money.

"We'll buy a new blanket for your bed," Mother said. "It's a wonder you don't freeze to death in the wintertime."

"I do," I said. We smiled at each other again. "And we'll buy a new blanket for Junior and Sterling, too, okay?" I asked.

"If you want to."

"Can I heat up your tea, Mother?"

"Thank you, Francie. Just a half a cup this time."

We waited and waited and finally Daddy came home. I rushed to meet him. "I had seven oh four for a nickel, Daddy."

"I know."

"Me and Mother been sitting here planning how we're gonna spend that money."

"Well, I don't have it yet, dumpling," Daddy said, sitting down heavily.

YORUBA'S CHILDREN

"No," Mother said, "you can't mean you didn't get Francie's money."

"It was on my slip," Daddy said.

"It's okay paying Jocko what we owe him out of my hits," Mother said, "but you can't mean he took all of Francie's money. Didn't you tell him it was Francie's?"

"What difference does it make who hits, it's all the same. I promised Jocko I'd pay back the money we borrowed for Junior's lawyer with my commissions and hits, and no, I didn't tell him it was Francie's money, I just put it on the account."

"Oh, Lord," Mother said.

"It's okay," I cried. "I don't care, Mother. Honest, I don't."

"I'm sorry, Francie," Daddy said, standing up and getting ready to go back out.

But Mother had the last word. "It was Francie's hit, Adam, not ours. It was Francie's hit."

Daddy didn't say anything, just went out the door, and I was sorry now I had hit the old number. As I got ready for bed I thought, it just wasn't my day for making money.

WE was in trouble with Madame Queen again. Daddy was working for the WPA cleaning out sewers, and one rainy day he came home barking like a hound dog.

"It's pneumonia," Mother said that night, worried.

"Don't be silly, Henrietta," Daddy said. "It's just a cold."

"Mr. Caldwell died of pneumonia," Mother said, "and he sounded just like you before he went."

"Well, I ain't going nowhere, so don't get your hopes up."

"How could you say a thing like that, Adam, when all I'm thinking about is your health?"

161

"Because with my life insurance I'm probably worth more dead than alive."

"Stop talking like a fool." Mother's voice was sharp. "Your insurance is only for five hundred dollars."

"That's what I said," Daddy sighed, "I'm worth more dead than alive."

The next morning Daddy went back to his sewer and that night he was talking out of his head with fever. Mother made him stay home the next few days and piled all the old coats we used for blankets on top of him and the room smelled of camphor ice and spirits of niter.

Madame Queen came to see what was going on. Since Daddy wasn't in Harlem Hospital, she felt he couldn't possibly have walking pneumonia. He seemed in perfect condition to her and she practically ordered him back to work.

"He ain't going to work in no damp sewers tomorrow," Mother told Madame Queen. "What you want him to do, slide all the way into the grave before you'll believe he's sick?"

Madame Queen wasn't used to Mother talking back to her like that and she got out of there fast. But she got back at us. When Daddy didn't go back to the WPA the next day and lost that job, Madame Queen refused to put us back on relief.

Mother didn't even ask Daddy this time if she could take on more day's work, she just did, and now she was gone all day every day except Sunday. Sometimes she did just general housecleaning, but at some of her places she had the laundry to do, too. Then she would come home and try to keep up with our messy house since I wasn't much help. I cooked the dinner every day and washed the dishes, but after I dropped a sheet into the backyard while trying to hang it on the line and burnt up one of Daddy's good shirts with the iron, I didn't have to help with the laundry no more. I wasn't very good at cleaning up the house either. Mother said I daydreamed too much and she could do it faster without my help so just get on out of her way.

When Daddy was well again, he started hanging out on the street corners trying to hit the single action since he wasn't collecting numbers for Jocko anymore. He said he had gotten too deep in the hole and wasn't making any money anyhow, so what was the point. And he played poker almost every night, sometimes not getting home at all.

Then Junior had to get smart and stay out all one night, celebrating because he got expelled from school for being absent. When he finally came home the following evening, Daddy was waiting for him.

"I'm too big to be whipped anymore," James Junior told Daddy when he was ordered to go and fetch the razor strop.

For a moment I thought Daddy would leap across the room and choke Junior to death or else have a fit and drop dead himself. But instead he gripped the edge of the table hard as if to keep it between him and Junior so he wouldn't go after him.

"You're right," Daddy said finally, "you're pretty goddamned grown. You been with that fancy woman I hear you're running around with?"

Junior stiffened with surprise, then avoiding Daddy's eyes he nodded. "Yeah, that's where I've been."

"You grown enough to be layin' up in some woman's bed," Daddy said, "you grown enough to support yourself. I'll take care of your butt long as you're in school, so either get back in somehow or go to work or move the hell out of here."

Junior didn't say a word, just went to his room and put

his shirt and pants and underwear in a paper bag and walked to the door.

"I'll come up sometime and bring you some money," he told Mother, then he was gone.

Mother had been worrying about James Junior all night and day and she seemed stunned. She sat down hard on a chair and rocked herself back and forth.

"He's gone?" she asked. "Is he really gone?"

"He'll be back," Daddy said, his voice quiet now. He walked to Mother and held her by the shoulders, making her sit still.

"He ain't a bad boy, Adam," Mother said, "he just don' like school, never did. And he runs with that gang 'cause he likes to be with his friends."

"He'll be back, Henrietta. Now you stop worrying. He don't know how tough it is out there in those streets. Soon's he gets a taste of what it's like to be on his own, he'll be glad to come home."

I looked at Sterling who was standing in the kitchen doorway. My lip trembled and he grabbed me. "Don't you start now, Francie. Don't you dare cry, you hear me?"

I nodded. I was too nervous to cry.

"Who's that fancy woman you all was talking about?" Mother asked.

"Just a girl," Daddy said. "Don't you worry about it. James Junior is old enough to have himself a girl, I guess." Daddy pulled Mother to her feet and led her to their room and we all went to bed.

The last thing I heard Daddy say was: "Don't cry, honey. Please don't cry. You mark my words, that boy'll be back home in a few days."

But Junior didn't come home, not to stay or to visit or to

give Mother any money. Guess he didn't have none to give. Sukie told me later that Alfred said Junior was living up on 135th Street with a woman named Belle who used to be one of Alfred's girls.

ELEVEN

NOW that Junior was gone everything seemed to get worse. Mother and Daddy were always snapping at each other, then Daddy stopped coming home altogether. He'd bank the fires late at night and start them up in the morning but he didn't come upstairs in between. When I wanted to see him I'd ask people in the street:

"Hey, you seen my father?"

"He just went down the street, Francie."

I would hurry down to 119th Street. "Hello, Mrs. Mackey, you seen my father?"

"He was in my house playing cards till just ten minutes ago, Francie. He left to see what the lead was."

Usually, though, I could find Daddy at Mrs. Mackey's place. She kept a running poker game going and sold pig feet and King Kong. When I found him there Daddy would introduce me to the other men around the table, then give me a quarter and send me home. I went looking for him at least once a week 'cause sometimes I got hungry just for the sight of him.

As soon as it turned warm the men started hanging out on our roof again, I guess because so many girls lived around there. Before, when we saw a man on the roof, we used to holler for our fathers or brothers and they would stick their heads out the windows and yell at them or run up there and those guys would beat it. But Daddy was never home now, Mr. Caldwell and Papa Dan were dead, Junior was gone, Vallie and Pee Wee were in jail and Sterling spent most of his time over at Michael's house messing around with their chemicals. Michael was the only other colored boy in Sterling's class at school and they had become tight buddies.

I liked Michael. He was light brown and had odd gray eyes and was real long legged, looming way over me, which was more than I could say for most boys 'cause I had shot up like an exploding firecracker and was getting too tall for a girl. And naturally, I was always falling over my big feet when Michael was around and couldn't find anything to say.

Once when he came by to study with Sterling and I opened the door for him, he smiled and chucked me under the chin.

"You're a cute kid, Francie. Remind me to fall in love with you when you grow up."

My whole body tingled and I dreamed about him for three whole days. But the next time I saw him he had forgotten all about me 'cause he just mumbled hello and kept on going. I still liked Michael, though, and got tongue-tied and nervous whenever he came by, which wasn't often, 'cause like I said he and Sterling spent most of their time over at his house.

Anyhow, those men on the roof had a field day. No more

white men turned up, though, just colored and Puerto Rican. At least once a week I'd knock on the Caldwells' window and whisper to Rebecca or Maude: "There's a man up there showing off his thing again," and we would sit in the window and watch him.

"Why do they like for us to see them do that?" I asked Rebecca once. It sure was nasty and I didn't think I was ever gonna let a man do it to me.

She shrugged. "Because they ain't normal, that's why."

"You ever let anybody do it to you, Becky?"

She didn't answer. Her eyes were glued to the man. Both of his hands were wrapped around his private and he was jerking on it so hard he looked like he had St. Vitus's Day Dance. Becky's tongue darted over her lips nervously. I turned away from her. I bet she *had* let somebody do it to her. I liked it better when I watched with Maude because she thought those men were nasty like I did. Although sometimes I didn't know about Maude either. She could say the darndest things, like yesterday when she was walking me over the roof.

"I'm never gonna get married," she said. "People fuss and fight all the time."

"Ain't it the truth," I said. "What you wanna be when you grow up, Maude?"

"A prostitute."

"Last year you said you was gonna be a nurse. Why you change your mind like that?"

"Because I want to, that's why."

"But how come you want to be a prostitute?"

"Because then you can get all you want but don't have to be married."

"You kiddin'?"

"Maybe I am and maybe I ain't."

Like I said, it was hard to tell about Maude sometimes.

AFTER dinner I headed for the bathroom to postpone my date with the dishes, but I had to come out of there in a hurry 'cause the air was so smoky it made me choke. Sterling had been in there again with his stinking chemicals. Whenever he wasn't over at Michael's house he was exploding things in our bathroom like nobody else had to use it except him.

I went into the kitchen. Sterling was sitting at the kitchen table studying. "Why can't Sterling do his experiments in his room?" I grumbled to Mother.

"Because he's got to sleep in there," Mother answered, "that's why. You want him to strangle to death?"

"Better him than me. I can't even read in the bathroom no more, can't see the print for the smoke."

"Good," Mother said, "you spend most of your time reading instead of helping me around the house. You gonna get addlebrained one of these days. Come on now and get these dishes done."

Sterling was ignoring me so as I passed him I asked: "What you and Michael making anyhow? A better grade of horse shit? That's what it smells like."

"Francie!" Mother aimed a backhanded slap at me but I ducked. "Stop using such language. You don't have to be so coarse. Say horse manure."

"Yes, Mother." I stuck my tongue out at Sterling and he thumbed his nose at me.

Then all of a sudden Sterling and Michael started playing hooky. Mother couldn't believe it when she found out, not Sterling, who was going to college and be our salvation.

"I'm tired of looking like a ragpicker at school," Sterling said, "and shining shoes for peanuts. I'm gonna get a job and make me some real money."

"But you like school," Mother said, bewildered. "You get good grades and study all the time."

"And for what? Okay, so I spend seven more years in school and get a degree. How many firms gonna hire a black chemist? They'll hardly hire a black janitor. I want to make some money *now,* Mother. I'm tired of taking your dimes and quarters and—"

"Don't do this, Sterling," Mother begged. "Please, don't do this to me."

Mr. Bryant, Michael's father, came over to see Daddy who wasn't home so he and Mother had a long talk. Mr. Bryant looked just like Michael, tall and with those strange gray eyes.

"What we gotta do," he told Mother, "is to keep our boys apart. They're both smart as a whip but when they're together for some reason they get the devil in them. Michael ain't never played hooky before."

"Neither has Sterling."

"I know. Now if we can keep them separated maybe we can knock out that stupid idea they got to quit school and find a job. Them boys have all the rest of their lives to work at some low-paying job reserved for ignorant niggers. They got to stay in school, they just got to."

"I always said Sterling was going to be the salvation of us all," Mother said. "My oldest boy, James Junior, never did well in school, not that he was stupid, but he just never got the feel of it. But Sterling's always been bright. But I don't know what to do. He's too stubborn to whip. If I thought it would do any good I'd whip him all the way down to that school and back, every day of the week. I'll talk to him some more, Mr. Bryant. I don't see how we can keep him and Michael apart but we can try, and thank you for stopping in to see me."

"Give my regards to your husband," Mr. Bryant said, and left.

Mother did try talking to Sterling again, every chance she got. Once when he shouted that the white kids at school dressed sharp and everything while he and Michael looked like pickaninnies I told him: "So who asked you to go downtown to a school where only white boys go? Why wasn't the high school for colored kids good enough for you?"

"You say one more word," Sterling offered, "and I'll slap the pee out of you."

"What's gotten into both of you," Mother cried, "that you use such language in front of me? And if I ever hear you talk to your sister like that again, Sterling, I'm gonna break your neck. You understand me?"

"Yes, Mother."

Then she started on him again, pleading. She only had a fifth-grade education and God knows she didn't want her children to have to work as hard as she did. But none of her talking did any good. Three weeks before summer vacation Sterling got a job with the undertaker across the street making seven dollars a week and quit school altogether.

When Daddy came home on one of his rare visits to give Mother a few dollars, she told him Sterling had finally made good his threat and found a full-time job.

Daddy sat down at the dining-room table, leaning his head in his hands. "How come a man's got to be plagued with sons like mine?" he asked. "I saw James Junior the other day on 118th Street and—"

"You didn't tell me you saw him," Mother interrupted. "Is he all right?"

"Yeah," Daddy said. "He's fine, I guess, from his standpoint. Wearing a brand-new suit and some pointed suede shoes. And know who he was with? That damn pimp, Alfred. I guess that's who he admires and wants to be like 'cause Alfred always has plenty of money, sports a diamond ring and a big car, and has contact with white people in high places. I asked him, son, you workin'? And he said no, not exactly, and I was scared to ask where he got his new clothes from. Then I told him he could come home anytime he wanted to, that this was always his home and the door was open. He said thanks, real politely, but he was doin' all right and he'd be up to see you soon."

"How come you didn't tell me you saw him?" Mother demanded.

"Because I was mad. Hanging around with that damn pimp and trying to be like him."

"You don't know he's tryin' to be like Alfred," Mother said.

"I do so know," Daddy hollered. "Didn't I see my boy with my own eyes aping that pimp?"

But Mother wasn't about to believe it, I could see that, and she just shut it out of her mind. I couldn't believe it either.

"And then I thought," Daddy continued quietly, "that one out of two ain't bad. Sterling was intelligent and going on to college. I would have got the money somehow, Henrietta, I swear. I would have stolen the money if need be to get Sterling in college. But if he don't wanna go, if his head is so hard he don't wanna finish school, then I'll be damned if I'm . . ." He broke off and stood up. "Make him give you four dollars a week for his room and board. If he won't stay in school he'll have to pay his own way."

Then he was gone, shaking his head and muttering that he was cursed with idiots for sons.

FINALLY it was summer and I was thirteen. I tried to get excited about it but it was just another ordinary day. Mother gave me a dime and I gave a nickel of it to Sukie. We did the same things we had always done, putting on our old bathing suits in the morning and walking up and down the streets looking for a johnny pump the boys had turned on. They put a wooden box over it making the water squirt up high and we'd get good and wet until a cop showed up and turned the hydrant off and then we'd wander around looking for another turned-on johnny pump. Or we would walk up to 131st Street and visit Aunt Hazel and she and Mr. Mulberry would fuss over us and feed us soda and cake till we almost popped. But nothing was too much fun anymore. I spent a lot of time reading on the fire escape, looking at the bell tower in Mt. Morris Park and then down the other way at the Empire State Building, very hazy in the distance. It seemed like Harlem was trapped in a valley between those two high points. I knew what was on the other side of the bell tower, more Harlem, but way down Fifth Avenue on the other side of the skyscrapers, that was another world, and I looked and sighed and dreamed that I was way over there instead of stuck here in my black valley.

At night I coaxed myself to sleep by imagining that Ken Maynard came charging down Fifth Avenue on his mighty white horse, and swooping me up in his arms, we rode off into that other world.

One day, though, I went to the Jewel Theatre and the

strangest thing happened. For a couple months now I had been noticing that cowboy pictures didn't send me like they used to. Not Tom Mix or Bob Steele or even Ken Maynard. This day, during the big battle when Ken was surrounded by Apaches who had set the covered wagons afire, I found myself rooting for the Indians. I didn't want them to get wiped out again, but the cavalry rode in just in the nick of time and those Indians were slaughtered like always. It made me mad. That white man who had broken the treaty with them was the real villain. He did get killed but it was too late, I was already on the wrong side and it was all spoiled.

I left the theater and walked slowly home feeling evil. I slipped on a banana peel and angrily kicked it off the curb where it found a home with a pile of garbage a storekeeper had just swept into the gutter. Seemed like Harlem was nothing but one big garbage heap. And how crowded the streets were, people practically falling off the sidewalks, kids scrambling between your legs almost knocking you down. There was something black and evil in these streets and that something was in me, too.

I was climbing the steps of my stoop when Max the Baker called me. The lights in the bakery were off.

"I was just getting ready to close," Max said as I went past him into the shop. Really, he was too chalk-white and tiny to be real. "I got a bag of cookies that will be stale by tomorrow," he said. "I thought you might like them."

They're already stale, I thought. Max don't give away nothing good. He held out the bag with one hand, covered with dark hair right down to the knuckles, while his other hand grabbed my shoulder and slid down to my breast. I brought up one knee and aimed it between his legs. It wasn't a good jab but I got part of him because he yelled, dropping the bag of cookies, and bent over double.

"Do it to your mother," I shouted, and ran outside. And tomorrow I'd get that lousy butcher and his extra pieces of rotten meat.

I went upstairs and found Mother in her bedroom patching my skirt which was so worn it was gonna look like a patchwork quilt.

"Mother, we ever gonna move off Fifth Avenue?"

She put the skirt down and looked at me for a long time. Finally she said: "One of these days, Francie, we gonna move off of these mean streets."

"HE asked me who you was," the Twin said, "and he wanted to know how old you were."

"What did you tell him?" I asked, excited.

The Twin looked at me like I was crazy. "I told him you was thirteen like you is. What did you expect me to tell him?"

"Then what did he say?"

"He said thirteen was kinda young, but you looked older so he still wants to meet you. He's sixteen."

"Sixteen," I said. "He don't look that old."

I had seen Vincent from a distance yesterday, a light handsome boy with good hair. He was the Twin's cousin visiting them from Florida.

"Anyway, he'll be down on the stoop with the gang tonight," the Twin said, "so come on down and meet him."

"Well, I don't know," I said. "I gotta lot of things to do upstairs."

"Like what? You scared of boys or something, Francie?"

"Don't be silly, Twin. I ain't scared," I lied.

As the Twin walked toward 118th Street, her fat butt
bouncing behind her, Sukie came up.

"Hello, Sukie."

"Hello, Francie. Let's go to the park."

"We goin' swingin'?" I asked.

"Nope."

"I don't wanna go then."

"What's the matter? You don't feel good or somethin'?"

"No, I just don't wanna go where those men are anymore."

Sukie's face turned red. "You signifying something bad
about me?"

"No, Sukie, I just don't wanna—"

"You know what? I ain't whipped your ass in a long
time."

"Sukie. How come you wanna talk like that?"

"You ready to fight now?"

I sighed and backed up. "No, Sukie. I can't fight today. I
ain't got time. I gotta go now." I ran inside my hall and up
the stairs. Well, I thought, I should have known she'd get
around to picking a fight with me again sooner or later.

I didn't go downstairs that night to meet Vincent but
stayed up on the fire escape almost falling over the railing
looking down at everybody on the stoop having a good
time. Maude and Rebecca were there and Sonny Taylor
and Duke from 119th Street and Sukie and the Twins and a
couple of other boys from Madison Avenue. They were
dancing on the tile in front of Max the Baker's. It wasn't on
account of Sukie that I didn't go down. She wouldn't pick a
fight with me in front of all those boys, I knew, but I was
scared to meet Vincent. What did you say to a handsome
light boy from Florida who had straight hair when you were
nappy-headed and black?

Sixteen. What a jazzy age, I thought, as I wrapped my arms about myself and imagined that it was Vincent's arms and we were dancing. We were lindying up and down on the tile, then we were in a glittering ballroom, me in a long gown, and we were waltzing to a big orchestra and everybody was watching us, we danced that good together.

We were going steady. Not right now, but next year when he came back. Of course he would come back. Nothing could keep him away from me.

"Nothing can keep me away from you, Francie, my darling," he whispered in my ear. "I'll carry you away from here. To Florida or even California. Anywhere you want to go. I love you."

I hugged myself again and wondered if I should go downstairs and meet him, but the thought of me stumbling all over myself kept me up on the fire escape. I looked over the railing again. He stood head and shoulders over the other boys and was lindying with Sukie now. He was a sharp dancer. The stars were very bright and low in the sky, like you could reach up and pluck one, and I sat there dreaming about me and Vincent and I hadn't been so happy since I don't know when.

For the next few days whenever Mother sent me to the store I was in agony. Suppose I met Vincent in the street or in the hallway? What would I say? I was so busy dodging Vincent that I forgot to be on the lookout for Sukie, and as I was coming back from the butcher one day, with no extra meat, there she stood with her moriney self.

"I can't fight now, Sukie, my mother's waiting for this meat."

"I got plenty of time."

"Yeah, I know," I sighed. "Say, I saw you dancing with Vincent the other night. You like him?"

"Naw, he thinks he's cute but he's an asshole."

I went into my hallway. Sukie was lying. Vincent wasn't an asshole and she knew it. She was just jealous because he liked me better than he did her.

On the fifth night I couldn't bear watching them have a good time without me no more and I finally went downstairs. They were laughing and joking on the stoop and I stood there for a long time before anybody noticed me.

"Hi, Francie," one of the Twins finally said.

Vincent didn't even look up. He was talking to Sukie, telling her a long story, too long, it seemed to me. Finally he finished and they both laughed.

"Hey, Francie," Maude yelled, "where you been all week? Hidin'?"

I could have kicked her. "I was busy studyin'," I mumbled.

"Studying in the summertime?" Vincent asked, in a high voice.

"She's backward like that," Sukie said, and everybody giggled.

I would have fainted if I knew how.

Vincent looked me up and down. "You sure are tall for a girl," he said. "I bet you're almost as tall as I am."

"Oh, no," I said, "I look taller than I am 'cause I'm so skinny, but I ain't . . ."

He wasn't listening. He had turned back to Sukie and was lighting a cigarette, not that straw we all smoked, but those skinny stinking things they smoked in the Apollo balcony. He was showing off. He inhaled deeply and passed the cigarette to Sukie. She puffed on it like she knew what she was doing and handed it back to him, showing off, too.

I smiled at nobody in particular until my face grew stiff,

then mumbling that I had to go, I fled back into the safety of the dark hall. I ran upstairs and went to bed.

I ain't too tall, I thought, and screw him. He wasn't different nohow from those stupid boys on the block always jivin' around and actin' the fool and going nowhere but to Sing Sing, like Daddy said. I didn't like light boys nohow, they were too stuck up. Screw you, Vincent. Screw you.

The next morning was one of those hot heavy days that make you feel like you're being squashed to the ground with a steamroller. I was so blue I went looking for Daddy.

"Have you seen my father, Slim Jim?"

"I just left him up at Mrs. Mackey's, Francie."

"Thanks." I walked to 119th Street and went to Mrs. Mackey's apartment. She opened the door.

"He's inside there, Francie."

I went into the bedroom and Daddy was laying across the bed asleep. "Daddy. Daddy."

"Hello, sugar." He hugged me. After we talked for a minute or two he called out to Mrs. Mackey: "Mabel, give Francie a quarter for me, will you? I'll give it back to you this afternoon."

Mrs. Mackey gave me the quarter and I left. When Mother came home from work that afternoon I told her about it. She was down on her hands and knees scrubbing the kitchen floor and she almost knocked over the basin of soapy water when I said Daddy had been laying on Mrs. Mackey's bed.

"He was in her bedroom, Francie? In her bed?"

"Yes, Mother. He didn't have a quarter so he . . ."

Mother was crying. She was still scrubbing the floor and the tears were rolling silently down her cheek. Back and forth her hand scrubbed the same spot.

"Mother." I was frightened. "Mother, please don't cry." Sterling came out of his room.

"Francie saw Daddy in Mrs. Mackey's bed," Mother told him, raising her eyes to meet his.

Sterling took the scrub brush out of her hand and gently pulling her to her feet, he led her to her bedroom. When I tried to follow he pushed me away, his face bunched up with anger. I waited outside the door and he came out in a little while.

"Don't you have no better sense than to tell everything you know?"

"What did I do?"

"Shut up. Don't start Mother off again." He pushed me ahead of him into the kitchen. He picked up the brush and started to scrub where Mother had left off.

"I only told her Daddy asked Mrs. Mackey to give me a quarter and . . ."

"And he was in her bed."

"Not in it, on it. I just mentioned that and she started to cry. Why would that make her cry?"

"Because he's living over there, that's why."

"Who," I asked stupidly, "Daddy? Mother thinks that Daddy and Mrs. Mackey . . ."

"She don't think, she knows, thanks to your big mouth."

"Sterling," I spoke very slowly, "is that why he don't come home no more? Because he's living with Mrs. Mackey?"

"Yeah, yeah, yeah. And stop tracking up this floor as fast as I wash it, will you? Get on out of here. And don't go in Mother's room and bother her."

I ignored Sterling and went in Mother's room. She was lying on the bed with her face turned to the wall. I went through to the front room and climbed out on the fire escape. It's not true, I thought, it's just not true.

Mother and I were alone that evening in the dining room when Daddy came upstairs. I went into the bedroom so they could be alone, but I sat on Mother's bed, listening.

"I had a little luck last night," Daddy said, "here's twenty dollars."

"Thanks," Mother said. "The rent was due last week, I'll pay it."

"That lousy Jew oughta give us all the rent free for being janitor," Daddy said, "instead of just half."

Mother didn't answer. Last month Daddy didn't bring her anything so she borrowed the rent money from Aunt Hazel.

"Well," Daddy said, "I gotta go."

I waited for Mother to tell him she knew about him and Mrs. Mackey but she didn't say a word, and I heard the door shut behind Daddy. I was stunned. Why was she letting him get away with it? I ran into the front room, out the door, and down the stairs, taking them two at a time. I caught up with Daddy when he was in the vestibule.

"Daddy."

I was standing on the first three steps so when he turned to me our eyes met.

"Yes, dumpling."

"You livin' with Mrs. Mackey, Daddy? That why you don't come home no more?"

His face fell apart, then tightened into angry lines. "Who been filling you with that crap? Your mother?"

It's true, I thought, Lord, it's true. I wanted to rush into his face and scratch it bloody. I wanted to hear him cry and turn *his* face to the wall. But I just stood there like I was turned to stone.

Daddy was muttering something. I was a little girl and couldn't understand, but I would someday. The silence grew between us, then with a big sigh, Daddy turned and went into the street. His movement unfroze me. I ran to the door and shouted at his back. "You forgot about Yoruba, Daddy. You forgot you was one of Yoruba's children."

Maybe he didn't hear me 'cause he kept on walking toward 118th Street. And Mrs. Mackey was a black bitch, I thought, and the next time I saw her I'd tell her so. I ran down the street in the opposite direction looking for Sukie. Goddammit, where was she? I raced down 117th Street to Lenox and over to 116th Street and back to Fifth Avenue. I finally found her on Madison Avenue jumping rope with some of the kids over there. I ran right up to her.

"You ready to fight now?" I asked, and before she could answer, I banged her in the nose.

Sukie backed up. "What the hell's the matter with you, Francie? You sick or somethin'?"

"No, I'm just ready to fight. Whose ass you say you was gonna whip?"

"You *are* sick," she said, "and I ain't fighting no sick people. I'll take care of your ass tomorrow," and she marched off before I got a chance to sock her again.

I walked aimlessly down to Central Park and sat on a rock throwing stones into the lake. I sat there until the trees melted into the shadows and the trunks turned into gaping jaws and the branches into writhing snakes. I got up and felt the panic clawing inside me, waiting to burst into a scream. I clamped my lips tightly together and ran down the path keeping as far away from the killer trees as possible. I made my way out of the park.

Sukie was going to fight me this night. I was tired of messing around with her. Fifth Avenue was crawling with people but Sukie was nowhere to be found. I went up to her apartment and banged on her door. No answer. I continued up to the roof, forgetting that I was afraid of the dark, and crawled down the ladder to her fire escape.

The window was open but it was dark inside. I was just about to holler for Sukie when I heard a noise. I laid down on the fire escape and raised my head above the sill. It was a bright moonlit night, but I couldn't see much. Then I heard a noise again, a grunt, and saw a flicker of light, just a spark for an instant, then it disappeared.

I heard Sukie's voice say: "No, no."

A man's deep voice mumbled something I couldn't understand. I could see their outlines now. They were on the couch in a dark corner of the room, but I couldn't see much. A light flickered again, and I heard that old couch thumping and squeaking.

Sukie is a sneak thief, I thought, pretending all the time she didn't like Vincent and planning all the while to let him do it to her. My heart was jumping about so I almost rolled off the fire escape. When the squeaking and groaning ended, I crawled past the window to the ladder, crossed over the roof, and went home.

"Francie, where you been?"

"Looking for Sukie, Mother."

"She home?"

I hesitated for only a moment. "No."

We pulled the sofa away from the wall and I climbed into it and began to scratch. The bugs had finally made it to our new couch. I hoped Sukie's mother would come home early and find them and throw both their butts out the window. But I wasn't really mad at Sukie. It was a strange feeling I had, an ache deep down somewhere, like everybody had gone off to some strange land and left me behind.

TWELVE

ON Sunday Mother and I went to church and she let me wear her good silk stockings. The ones she wore were so runny they looked like net and I noticed for the first time how turned over her heels were.

Adam talked about boycotting the stores on 125th Street until they hired colored people and announced there was gonna be a meeting in the church basement that night to plan it. Then he got down to preaching.

At the end of his sermon while the choir was singing softly in the background, "Take your burdens to the Lord and leave them there," and Adam was standing up in the pulpit with his arms outstretched, looking handsome and near white, asking the sinners to come forth and be saved, Mother started to shout.

"Jesus, help me. O Lord, Lord, Lord." She stiffened in her seat, flinging her arms up over her head, crying out loud for God's mercy.

Mother, don't. Somebody. Help my mother. The nurse came running. Everybody close by turned around to look at us but I didn't care. She had a right to cry and shout like everybody else, didn't she? I glared at the starers but they were nodding at Mother in sympathy.

"It's all right, sister. He knows how much you can bear."

"Amen, I say. Amen."

The nurse wiped Mother's sweating forehead and suddenly she was herself again and avoiding my eyes. I leaned forward, hesitated a moment, then kissed her cheek.

"I'm all right, Francie."

"Yes, Mother." I turned my attention back to Adam.

"We will now sing hymn number two eighty-two," he said, " 'Leaning on the Everlasting Arms.' "

I made a mental note of the number along with everybody else so I wouldn't forget to play it tomorrow.

That afternoon I saw Sukie for the first time since I peeked in on her and Vincent from the fire escape.

"Hello, Sukie."

"Hi."

"You wanna fight?" I asked, my heart not really in it.

"Naw," Sukie said. "We're too old to be fighting like children. We got better things to do."

"Yeah," I agreed. I waited for her to tell me what better things she had been doing and when she didn't, I asked her. "What better things you been doing, Sukie?"

"What you mean?"

"You said we had better things to do than fight so I thought you meant something special. Like maybe you had something to tell me."

"What I got to tell you?"

"How do I know what you got to tell me?"

"I ain't got nothin' to tell you."

"Oh, for christsake," I said. So she was gonna be selfish and keep it a secret from me. Vincent had gone back to Florida so why wouldn't she tell me what happened?

"What you wanna do?" I asked.

She shrugged.

"Let's walk down to 112th Street," I suggested.

We started out silently. I looked at her sidewise but she didn't seem any different than before. You would think it would show in some way, but it didn't. There she was, spitting into the gutter like always, looking pretty and evil all at the same time.

At the corner of 115th Street a street speaker was up on a ladder as usual in front of a small crowd. As we drew closer we were surprised to discover that it was Robert. He stood on the second rung, his elbow resting on the top of the ladder and frowning down on the people like they were his enemies.

"The Italians in this country know how to throw *their* weight around," he hollered. "They got influence and can pressure businessmen here into helping Italy. America says it's neutral but why is Roosevelt still shipping oil to Mussolini? Oil which helps him kill black people? Answer me that. I'll tell you why. It's because Italian Americans got political and economic power, that's why. And what kind of power do black people have? What are we doing to help Ethiopia? What are we doing to help ourselves? I tell you, brothers and sisters, the black man in this country must make his own life. The crying Negro must die. The cringing Negro must die. If he don't kill hisself the environment will, and we been dying for too long. The man who gets the power is the man who develops his own strength. I ain't talking about strength in his muscles but in his mind. We got to get a better education. We got to build Negro economic and political freedom. And if we don't, in fifty years from now, or sooner, this country will be bloody with race wars."

"He keep that up he gonna get hoarse," Sukie said. "If

Elizabeth could see him up on the ladder hollering like a fool, she'd quit him."

"He ain't no fool," I said, suddenly angry. "They're the fools." I pointed to the restless crowd. "They're just listening 'cause they ain't got nothing else to do since there's no numbers to play today. Why don't they *do* something?"

"Like what?"

"Like what Robert is saying."

"He ain't saying shit."

"He is so," I yelled.

"Francie, you out of your mind hollering at me like that?"

I swallowed hard. I must be out of my mind. "I'm sorry, Sukie." I turned back to Robert who was talking more calmly now.

"Having had the wrong education in this country from the start," he said, "we are our own greatest enemy. Marcus Garvey said that in the twenties and it's still true. But it don't have to be that way. Did you know that while white people were still running around in caves in Europe, like the barbarians they still are, that Africans were emperors and kings of civilized empires? Did you know that Timbuktu had a great university and was the main stem for learning way back in the ninth century? Check it out, brothers and sisters. And don't you believe the white man when he tells you that you never had a pot or a window."

The crowd tittered. A few men close up nodded their heads in agreement, but most of the others just looked off, only half listening.

We *didn't* have a pot to piss in or a window to throw it out of, I thought, so who could believe what Robert was saying? I never read anything in school about black kings and junk like that. The only people who ever said such things was Daddy and street speakers like Robert. And suppose what they said was true? How could it help us now anyway?

Me and Sukie walked on down to 112th Street and stared at the clothes and stuff in Woolworth's window. If the store had been opened we could have gone inside and swiped a cookie, but everything was dead on Sunday, so we just stood there and listened to the Puerto Ricans passing by talking to each other in Spanish.

Suddenly I wished I could speak Spanish, or anything, and if I had to be black, why couldn't I at least have been Puerto Rican?

A couple of days later I was sitting on my stoop doing nothing when Rachel called me from the candy store.

"Francie, will you go to the drugstore for me?"

"Sure, Rachel, what you want?"

"Come inside a minute."

As I entered the store I noticed a poster in the window advertising the Joe Louis-Max Baer fight at Madison Square Garden next month. I hoped Joe would beat him blind.

Rachel took a quarter from the cash register and handed it to me. "Here, I'll write down what I want."

"I can remember."

"I know, but just in case there are people around you hand the note to the druggist, see?"

I didn't see, but I took the note and the money to the druggist and he gave me a square box already wrapped. I knew what was in it. Kotex. I was still using rags but Rebecca had given me one of her Kotex pads once and she took it out of a box just like this with the wrapping paper still on it. I pushed open the candy store door and handed the box to Rachel.

"Take what you want," she said, indicating the row of two-cent candies.

When I went to the store for her father or mother they always let me choose from the five-cent candy. I noticed now that Rachel wasn't as pretty as she used to be 'cause she was getting too fat. Too chalky white with a round rouge spot on each cheek and too fat. I picked out a peanut bar.

"Francie, I was wondering if you would like to clean for us tomorrow. No heavy work, just a little dusting and washing dishes and things like that for maybe five hours and make yourself a dollar."

"Yeah, Rachel, I think I can do it." I didn't like to wash dishes, but for a dollar I would pretend.

I raced upstairs. "Mother, Mother, I got a job."

She grunted and didn't seem too impressed.

After breakfast the next morning, which was Saturday, I started out, very excited. I walked down to 110th Street and found the address right across the street from Central Park. It was a nice white stone building. The hallway was clean and had a different smell than the ones in Harlem, strong cooking odors, but not the same as ours. I took the elevator up to the tenth floor. Rachel and her mother were home. The apartment was bright with big rooms and the funny smell was stronger inside. I found out what it was—gefilte fish.

"In the kitchen, that's where we start, Francie," Mrs. Rathbone said, leading me down the hall. She was very short and white-haired with a thick accent. "Dirty dishes we got plenty," she said cheerfully.

She wasn't foolin'. It looked like they had been cooking for months, there were that many dishes and pots in the sink. It took me over two hours to get them all washed and put away. Then Rachel brought me a pan of soapy water and a brush and I scrubbed the kitchen floor.

"Don't miss that spot under the sink, Francie," she said.

Mrs. Rathbone handed me a carpet sweeper and I did the rugs in the living and dining rooms and in the hallway. Rachel was waiting for me with another bucket of water by the front-room window. She held out a rag and pointed to the window. I had seen my mother cleaning the outside of a window by sitting on the sill, half of her inside and half of her outside. That was what Rachel was telling me to do now.

I opened the window and felt a blast of cool air but that wasn't what bothered me. I looked down ten stories.

"I'm scared to sit outside that window, Rachel," I told her.

"Francie, don't worry, I'll hold you," she said.

She stuck the rag in my hand and I sat on the sill. Rachel pulled the window down to my lap. Holding on to the bottom of the window with one hand, with the other I dabbed at the pane with the rag, almost crying. Rachel was holding me all right. She was pinching a tiny piece of my dress between her thumb and forefinger like it was dirt. I did both front windows, then dusted the furniture in the bedroom. I had been there seven and a half hours. Rachel gave me a dollar and asked if I could come back next Saturday. I didn't even answer her. I ran out of the house and went home.

When Mother came in from work I gave her the dollar.

"Was it hard, Francie?" she asked smiling. "It couldn't

have been easy seeing as how I can't get you to do a thing around here."

"It was all right," I said, "except washing the windows. I told Rachel I was scared to sit on the outside and she said she'd hold me, but Mother, she just held on to a little piece of my dress."

"Rachel had you washing windows?"

"Yes, Mother. That's what I said."

"You come with me."

Mother ran down the whole five flights of stairs and burst into the candy store. Nobody was there but Mr. Rathbone. Mother marched right behind the counter.

"Damn you," she said as Mr. Rathbone backed his plump behind up into the soda fountain. It was the first time I'd ever heard her curse. "You tryin' to kill my child? She don't have to wash no windows for you, you hear? That's man's work. You outta your head making my child wash windows?"

"Mrs. Coffin, please. I don't know what . . ."

"You tell your wife and that fat daughter of yours that it's a good thing I can't get my hands on them right now. A good thing, you hear?"

For a minute I thought Mother might bust Mr. Rathbone in the nose in place of his fat daughter, but she turned away and we went back upstairs.

"You don't have to do no domestic work for nobody, Francie." We was in the kitchen fixing dinner. "You don't be no fool, you hear? You finish school and go on to college. Long as I live you don't have to scrub no white folks' floors or wash their filthy windows. What they think I'm spending my life on my knees in their kitchens for? So you can follow in my footsteps? You finish school and go on to college. Somebody in this family got to finish school. You hear what I say?"

"Yes, Mother, I hear."

Her face was red and sweating as she banged the pots around, grumbling under her breath. I was surprised at her anger which made me feel kinda sad, not because I had caused all this commotion, that made me feel important, but because she was my mother and I loved her but I suddenly realized I almost didn't know her at all.

LABOR Day couldn't come soon enough with school a week behind. I was tired of summer with nothing to do but read on the fire escape or go to the movies when I could hustle up a dime or wander up and down the streets with Sukie. Although I brought up Vincent's name several times, she ignored me and I finally stopped thinking about it altogether because her keeping it a secret from her very best friend hurt me.

Then it was autumn and the trees in the park had golden leaves sailing to the ground, but the weather was still hot and sticky like it didn't know any better.

One morning when me and Maude were walking to school she started crying, making no effort to wipe away the tears like she didn't care who saw them.

"They gonna kill them," she said. "They gonna keep messin' around but in the end they gonna kill them."

I knew what she was talking about. We heard it through the grapevine first, like we heard most everything else, and then it was in the papers. Governor Lehman said he wasn't about to change the death sentence for boys under twenty-one. He said he couldn't see no difference between the guilt of a man and a boy, so that petition the white folks sent to him wasn't gonna save a soul. There was ten boys waiting in the death house in Sing Sing, counting Vallie and the Washington brothers, and now they wouldn't have long to wait.

"What did Robert say?" I asked Maude.

"Said we was still appealing 'cause they beat Vallie and them to make them confess." She swallowed a sniffle. "That's against the law, you know, beating them in jail like that."

"I know," I said.

"But they don't care." She rocked from side to side on her bowlegs which was the way she walked. I used to be glad her legs were bowed, 'cause mine was so skinny and long and hers were worse looking. But now I was sorry I ever had such a nasty thought and I wished her legs were straight and pretty like Sukie's even if mine stayed ugly like they was surely apt to do.

"I know they gonna do it," she said. "They gonna electrocute my brother."

"Don't say that, Maude," I said. "You gotta have faith." That's what Mother had told Mrs. Caldwell so I said it again, as much to keep me from crying as to help Maude 'cause deep down I felt just like she did.

DAMN if he didn't do it. He beat the Butcher Boy. Everybody poured out of their houses to celebrate like it had been planned that way, me and Sterling among them. We'd listened to the fight with Mother in her bedroom on a radio she had bought a few months ago for two dollars down and a dollar a week which meant whenever the collection man from the store on 125th Street could catch her.

Yelling over the roar of the crowd, the referee had just declared Joe Louis the winner. Sterling jumped up and headed for the door with me at his heels.

"Don't let your sister out of your sight," Mother hollered

as we galloped down the stairs. I thought I heard Sterling mutter something under his breath, but I wasn't sure.

By the time we reached Lenox Avenue the streets were jammed.

"We did it," a brown boy shouted, flinging his cap up in the air and grabbing me around the waist. We did a two-step in the gutter. Sterling and a girl with a mouthful of buck teeth joined hands with us and we went round and round yelling and laughing until we collapsed in a dizzy heap on top of one another.

"We beat the shit out of that white boy, didn't we?" a tall yellow man demanded, and the crowd roared back:

"We beat him. We beat him. Joe Louis naturally whipped his razzamatazz. Whipped him so his mammy wouldn't know him."

Strangers hugged me and I squeezed them back. It was good to feel their touch. Good to yell at the top of my voice: "Long live the Brown Bomber."

The crowd spilled off the pavement into the street, stalling cars, which honked good-naturedly and then gave up as the riders jumped out and joined us lindying down the middle of Lenox Avenue.

Then I saw Junior and yelled at him. He ran forward to meet us. His arms reached out and I stumbled into them as he swung me off my feet and hugged me tight.

"James Junior, James Junior, where you been?" I kissed him, trying to see if he looked all right. He seemed to have growed some and looked nice in his new suit.

"Francie, little sister. Ain't this a glorious night?" He turned to Sterling and they hugged each other. "Man, did you hear how Joe Louis knocked that cat out? With a one-two and a right cross." Junior aimed his fist at Sterling's chin. Sterling ducked and came up inside Junior's arms, punching him lightly in the stomach.

"No, man," Sterling said, "this is the way he did it. First in the breadbasket, then the right cross." His fist landed on the side of Junior's head.

"If you say so," Junior said, rubbing his chin. They fell out laughing. "How's Mother—and Daddy, too?"

"They's both fine, James Junior," I answered, "but how come you never come home? You know Mother worries about you. How come you don't come home sometime like you said you would?"

He looked away from me. "Tell Mother I'm comin' to see her one day next week and bring her some money. You tell her that for me, Francie, okay?"

"Okay, Junior, but you know she don't care about no money."

"I know, little sister," he said softly, "but I care."

"Where'd you get your new suit?" Sterling asked.

"Somebody gave it to me. Sharp, ain't it?" He whirled around and I nodded.

Sonny had come up while we was talking. "You ready, man?" he asked Junior. "We're late."

"Yeah," Junior said, "let's go."

"Where you goin'," I asked, hopin' maybe he'd let me come, too.

"We got a job to do," Sonny said, clearly trying to get James Junior away from us.

"What kind of job you talkin' about, man?" Sterling asked.

Junior shrugged and started singing a street song: "Ask me no questions and I'll tell you no lies 'cause a man got hit with a bowl of shit and that's the reason why."

"Come on, man," Sonny said. "Alfred's waiting for us."

Junior cuffed me on the chin and walked off with Sonny.

"Ain't that good? James Junior's got a job," I said. "Mother will be so—"

"Shut up," Sterling cut me off. "And don't even mention to Mother that we saw him."

"But why, Sterling? How come I gotta—"

"Because I said so, that's why. Come on, let's go home."

He spoiled everything, Sterling did. The crowd was still making a joyful racket as we walked home silently, but now we were separated from the magic we had been a part of just a few moments ago.

IT was storming, one of those reddish days that looks like the earth's on fire. It got darker and darker, all in the middle of the day, like the sun had gone off somewhere and died. The rain came down with a roar. The thunder boomed, the lightning cracked across the sky, and as I pressed my nose against the living-room window looking out at the storm, I shivered just a little, for who could tell that this wasn't doomsday. Gabriel, Gabriel, blow on your horn and all ye dead rise up to be judged.

But instead, the storm disappeared like it had never been, and the old sun sailed back into the sky. The puddles dripped into the sewers and the pavement dried in minutes with only a round damp spot here and there to remind us it had rained.

The streets which had emptied with the sudden storm filled up again as quickly, and all was as before except that Harlem's face was a little cleaner. But all wasn't exactly the same, I found out later, because it was during that storm that China Doll did it. It wasn't until after dinner that the news hit Harlem with the same speed almost as that lightning bolt had tore across the sky.

I had gone over to the Caldwells' house and was sitting on the floor with Maude playing jacks when Rebecca came upstairs and rushed into the room. Elizabeth's two little boys were giving me and Maude a fit, grabbing the ball and jacks, messing up our game, and Mrs. Caldwell was ironing in a corner of the room.

"They done arrested China Doll," Rebecca said, all out of breath like she had run up the whole flight of stairs.

"Lord, what now?" Mrs. Caldwell said, putting down her iron.

"She stabbed Alfred," Rebecca said.

"She stabbed who?" I whispered, scared I had heard her right and wondering where Sukie was.

"Alfred, her pimp," Rebecca said. "China Doll got him with a butcher knife. Right in the heart. He's dead."

THIRTEEN

I RAN over the roof to Sukie's house and banged on her door. She answered it, her face swollen, her eyes red.

"You heard?" she asked.

I nodded as I walked past her into the dining room.

"He was always beatin' on her," Sukie said, "the bastard. She should have killed him long ago."

"Well, she finally done it," I mumbled, not knowing what else to say. But it was hard to believe that China Doll had stabbed him and was in jail. Sukie didn't offer to tell me anything more and I didn't want to seem nosy and ask her so we just sat there silently waiting for her mother to come home. When we heard her footsteps, Sukie went to the door and opened it.

"They told me downstairs," Mrs. Maceo said. "Soon's I get my breath I'll go on down to the jail. You eat yet?"

Sukie shook her head. "I ain't hungry."

Mrs. Maceo fell down into a chair, her moriney face pulled into a tighter frown than usual.

"Hello, Mrs. Maceo."

"Francie. That you?"

"Yes, ma'am."

"I'm sorry, Francie, I didn't see you. There you are, sitting right before me bigger than life and I didn't see you."

Then to my horror she started to cry, her face crumpling up like tissue paper, as if not seeing me had set her off. Sukie ran to her mother and fell on her breast but Mrs. Maceo pushed her away.

"I want you to remember this day," she said, her voice harsh. "It wasn't enough for your sister to be a no-good whore. No. She had to go and kill that pimp, too. Kill him. But she never would listen to me. Never heard a word I said. Now you see what a bad end she done come to. And you, miss, you're trying to step right into her shoes, I can see that already. You're hardheaded just like your sister. Hardheaded and sassy. Won't go to school, won't learn nothing. You're a trial to me, Sukie, a trial."

Sukie backed away from her mother. She slid into the wall, pushing herself into a corner like she was trying to climb to the other side.

"You gonna put me in my grave too before my time?" her mother asked. "You gonna be a no-good whore like your sister?"

"No," Sukie whispered, shaking her head violently. "No. No!"

Mrs. Maceo sighed. "I ain't got nothin' but my children and sometimes they's more than I can bear." She turned her eyes, dry now, on me. "Francie, run home and ask your mother if she'll go to the jail with me in about a half hour."

As I went out the door I tried to avoid looking at Sukie huddled in the corner, chewing on her bottom lip to keep from crying. I crossed over the roof and ran down the stairs to our apartment. I pushed against the door but it wouldn't open.

"Mother," I screamed in sudden panic. "Mother. Mother." I didn't even know if she was home from work yet, but in a moment she opened the door.

"What is it, Francie? What's the matter?"

I rushed past her. "The door wouldn't open. I pushed and pushed." I swallowed and the lump in my throat went away and with it the urge to scream. "Alfred's dead," I said as I followed Mother into the kitchen. "China Doll done killed him."

"I know. Mrs. Caldwell told me through the window soon's I came home. That's why you was screamin'? I thought somebody was chasin' you or somethin'."

"I . . . I just got scared. The door wouldn't open."

"You know it sticks sometime. What scared you?"

I shook my head. "I don't know. Nothin'."

We looked at each other and for a moment I thought she was gonna hug me. We swayed toward each other but neither of us swayed hard enough. Finally, I said: "Mrs. Maceo wants you to go to the jail with her. In a half hour."

"All right," Mother said. She passed a hand over her eyes for a moment, and I thought, she's tired, she's always tired, but I never heard her say so.

After she left I sat on the fire escape leaning against the brick wall and shivering, although it was a warm Indian summer night. I pulled my legs up to my chest and thought about poor China Doll cooped up in jail. Why *had* she killed Alfred? He had whipped her before and she hadn't killed him. Had he beaten her up again? I remembered her black eye and those scratches on her face that time. Then a dark thought came to me, so horrible it made me want to throw up. I ground my fists in my eyes and banged my head against the wall, trying to knock some sense in me. But I couldn't shut that thought out. I couldn't still the sound of

China's voice telling Alfred to keep his evil eye off her sister.

I remembered that spark of light I had seen while peeking through Sukie's window. Vincent didn't have no diamond ring to catch the light of the moon. I banged my head up against the wall again. No. No. It couldn't be. I *was* getting addlebrained just like Mother always said I would.

Again I saw that flash of light in the darkness and heard the man's low voice. Vincent's voice was high, wasn't it? It was Alfred who always spoke in a low rumble. And Sukie would have told me about it right away, showing off, if she had been with Vincent. That's why she kept it a secret, because it wasn't Vincent. It was . . .

A stranger. A stranger with a deep voice like Alfred's and a diamond ring. My heart stopped it's frantic pounding and I shuddered with relief. That was it.

I felt dizzy and came inside from the fire escape and went to bed, not even bothering to pull the couch away from the wall. I lay there, absentmindedly smashing bedbugs. Yes, that was it all right. A strange man had been with Sukie, and in the morning I would ask her who he was.

"Who was he, Sukie?"

"Alfred," she said. "Duke, Sonny, Slim Jim, Pee Wee, Max the Baker, Vincent. Your daddy."

She laughed and her teeth turned into a sparkling diamond ring which kept turning off and on like a neon light, off and on to the sound of her crazy laughter.

I woke up, frightened, and didn't go back to sleep until long after Mother came home.

Who was it, Sukie? Who was it? Every time I saw her I silently asked that question. But I knew she was never going to tell me. She had gone away somewhere inside herself, and she'd never tell me anything anymore.

They was still holding China Doll. Alfred *had* hit her again and everybody said he was too lowdown even for a pimp and how low down can you get?

About a week later I was walking down 118th Street just wandering around, when I saw Daddy. He fell in step with me and we walked on down to Fifth Avenue.

"How you been, Francie?"

"Just fine, thank you."

"Do you want to go to the show? I got a quarter I think I can spare."

"No, thank you."

"Your mother all right?"

"Yes, thank you."

"Tell her I'm gonna try and bring her the rent money tomorrow. I got a hunch seven twenty-two's gonna play today and I got a dollar on it."

I didn't answer him. When we got to the corner I waited to see which way he was turning and I started in the other direction.

"Francie."

I sighed loudly. "Yes?" but didn't turn around.

"You sure you don't wanna go to the show?"

"I'm sure, thank you," and I walked away.

Ever since that time I had followed him down the stairs I wouldn't take any money from him but he acted like nothing was wrong and kept trying to give me a quarter and once even a whole dollar, but I refused it politely, and I never went looking for him anymore either.

He wasn't the only one acting like nothing had happened. Only last week when Sterling made some sassy remark about Daddy not living there no more and good riddance, Mother grabbed him. She spun him around so fast and slapped his face so hard he was stunned. "Your father is still the head of this house," she told him, holding on to his shoulder and looking him straight in the eye, "and as long as you live you will respect your father."

I walked on down the street for half a block, then turned around and watched Daddy trudging down the avenue. Somehow, he didn't seem as big as he used to, and it wasn't until later I realized that he hadn't hollered at me for being in 118th Street and run me out.

SATURDAY I was looking out the front-room window when the strangest feeling hit me. It was too cold to sit on the fire escape so I was leaning on the windowsill looking at the boys across the street in front of the drugstore. They was acting the fool as usual, their knickers hanging loose, their caps on backward, whistling at the girls and falling out at their own jokes. As I watched them they didn't seem so bad all of a sudden, just full of fun, and I didn't want them to fall off the roof or cut each other or be hauled off to jail but just to stay there, safe and sound forever, laughing in front of the drugstore. I forgave them for making me hate to walk past them while they shouted:

"Shake that thing. Lord, look at that child walk."

"She's got a naturally educated behind."

"Little brown baby, ain't you got some sweet lovin' for me?"

I wanted to hug them all. We belonged to each other somehow. I'm getting sick, I thought, as I shifted my elbows on the windowsill. I must of caught some rare disease. But that sweet feeling hung on and I loved all of Harlem gently and didn't want to be Puerto Rican or anything else but my own rusty self.

That night when I went to bed I closed my eyes and heard the hoofbeats in the distance coming closer. "Here I am," I whispered. He rode up in the moonlight, and bending down from his horse, pulled me up onto the saddle. But it wasn't Ken Maynard. For weeks now when I put myself to sleep dreaming about my hero his features had been getting dimmer and dimmer. Now Ken Maynard was gone forever and my rider was faceless and didn't have no color at all. We rode down Fifth Avenue, past Central Park and the Empire State Building, and up into the moonlight. But no matter how hard I tried in the weeks and months to come, I couldn't fill in his features or make him either white or black.

IT was on the radio and when I went downstairs in the morning it was splashed all over the newspaper on Mr. Rathbone's stand. The racketeers had shot down Dutch Schultz and three of his henchmen. They was all dead or dying. I stood outside the candy store and read the story slowly, turning the page when it continued, 'cause it was more exciting than a movie. Then Mr. Rathbone came outside and said I shouldn't muss up his paper if I wasn't going to buy it, but I had finished reading it by then so I folded the newspaper back up and handed it to him with a sweet smile. He had stopped saving his day-old papers for me after Mother chewed him out that time about his fat daughter, Rachel.

When Sterling came home for lunch, I gave him a blow by blow description of how Dutch Schultz had been sitting in a tavern in New Jersey when he got his. I felt like we knew old Dutch, since he was head of the numbers and all.

"You think them gangsters gonna come and shoot up Jocko's store maybe, Sterling?"

He bit into the potted-meat sandwich I had fixed for him and looked at me darkly as if the food pained him somewhere. "You sure sound bloody, Francie. Why'd anybody want to shoot up Jocko?"

"I didn't say anybody would, I only asked if maybe the gangsters would be fightin' over the numbers racket and . . ."

"You don't read the papers very good," Sterling said, "else you'd know that a guy named Lucky something or other done took over the numbers from Dutch Schultz months ago ever since Dewey been trying to send old Dutch up the river."

"You already read about it?" I asked. "How come you let me tell you all that crap if you've already read it?"

"Because I was too tired to tell you to shut up."

"The undertaker let you read while you're suppose to be workin'?"

"He don't *let* me, I just do."

"I would think you'd be so scared of all them dead bodies lying around that you wouldn't take your eyes off of them for a minute."

"I ain't scared of nothin' living or dead and stop pesterin' me, will you?"

Somebody knocked at the door.

"Go answer it," Sterling said.

It was the white salesman from the jewelry store, a freckle-faced big man who said he came to collect on the radio.

"My mother ain't home," I said.

"Well, then, I'll have to repossess the radio," he said, pushing the door open wider and coming in.

"Sterling," I hollered.

Sterling came into the dining room. "What you want?" he asked the man.

"He said he gotta repossess the radio," I told him.

"You're two weeks past due in your payments," the man said, "and it's the policy of our store to—"

"You mean you think you gonna walk in here and take our radio just like that?" Sterling asked.

"Unless you pay up the arrears right now, I'll be forced—"

"You'll be forced to fall down all five flights of those stairs and break your fool neck if you take one step further," Sterling said. "I been paying two dollars a week on that radio myself for the past three months and it ain't worth a dime more. In fact, it ain't worth half of that."

"Your mother signed a contract agreeing to pay two dollars a week for—"

"For the rest of her life?" Sterling asked.

I had often seen Daddy threaten to throw white people down the stairs if they didn't get out of his house, like the time the electric man came to read the meter and caught the jumper in and wanted five dollars or he would rat on us, but this was the first time I had seen old Sterling in action, and he was just as good as Daddy. When he got through ranting and raving, that salesman turned beet-red and raced back down those stairs under his own steam.

Sterling shut the door and dusted off his hands. He looked at me and we both burst out laughing.

"Francie," he said, and when he smiled like that he looked just like James Junior, "today we own us a ra-di-o."

CHINA Doll was finally released. Justifiable homicide, they said. Sterling explained that meant you could protect yourself if somebody was beating you.

I went looking for Sukie to tell her the good news. Maybe we should go around the block and welcome China Doll home. I walked up and down the streets looking for Sukie and when I got back to her stoop I found her sitting there, elbows on her knees, her head propped in her hands.

"Hey," I yelled, "they let China Doll go."

"Yeah, I know," Sukie said, not looking up.

"Ain't you glad?" I asked. Then I noticed that she was crying.

"I wish they had kept her in jail forever," she said.

My heart stopped beating. "Why?" I whispered. "Because she killed Alfred?"

"No. Who cares about that bastard? He never shoulda been born."

"Then why, Sukie? Why?"

"Because everybody thinks I'm gonna be just like her. That's all my mother ever tells me. And I'm not gonna be like her, Francie. I ain't gonna be no whore."

"I don't think you gonna be a whore, Sukie."

"You ain't grown. You don't count."

"Move over," I said, and sat down beside her. There was nothing else to say. Either you was a whore like China Doll or you worked in a laundry or did day's work or ran poker games or had a baby every year. We sat there, Sukie rubbing her nose with the back of her hand and sniffling and me getting ready to join her any minute.

Sterling walked up. "What you two dopes sitting here crying for?" he asked.

"Sukie don't wanna be no whore like China Doll and I don't like livin' around here no more. I hate it."

"Move over," Sterling said, and sat down between us.

The sun was sinking fast and soon a dusty blanket of darkness would settle over the avenue, hiding some of its filth, but not all. The street was filled with colored people scurrying in and out of doorways, coming and going, crowding each other off the sidewalk. It was all too depressing. James Junior hadn't come to see Mother like he promised and I guess he didn't have a job after all, at least not an honest one. Vallie and them were going to get the electric chair and if they did get an appeal they'd be behind bars the rest of their life, so what was the difference? And Daddy didn't come home anymore.

I tried to get again that nice feeling I had for all of Harlem a few weeks ago, but I couldn't. We was all poor and black and apt to stay that way, and that was that.

"Mother says we're gonna move off of Fifth Avenue one of these days," I said, turning to Sterling.

He grunted something under his breath, then said it out loud.

"Shit."

The word hung between us in the silence. Then I sighed and repeated it.

"Shit."

Afterword

Daddy Was a Number Runner is the single fictional account in our literature of a year in the life of a young, black, adolescent girl, growing up in Harlem in the middle of the Great Depression. This fact alone gives it major historical importance, for the time was one that left deep and lasting impressions on Afro-Americans as well as all other Americans who lived through it. Within the female tradition that this book represents, it shares similarities with and divergences from Paule Marshall's *Brown Girl, Brownstones* (1959), a novel that explores some of the experiences of another black girl coming to early womanhood, but in the Bedford Stuyvesant section of Brooklyn, toward the end of the same period.

While *Daddy Was a Number Runner* is not autobiographical, it speaks to conditions that the author observed when she was a child. Sociological and historical studies of Harlem and the making of the black ghetto, with their statistics on crime and deviance, and their psychological profiles of juvenile delinquents and runaway fathers, appear almost meaningless as we become intimate with the flesh-and-blood people in *Daddy Was a Number Runner*. The data such documents provide are an inadequate measure of the feelings, strengths, weaknesses, triumphs, and failures of people whose laughter and tears are of equal intensity, both welling up from the very core of their beings. As readers, critics, and outsiders, we are unable to pass judgment on the people or the circumstances in this novel by separating them into categories clearly defined as good and bad or right and wrong; not even when we consider such widely divided issues as the ambiguous illegality of playing the numbers, or the moral and judicial ramifications of a mugging that results in a man's death. But we leave this book with a better understanding of the challenges presented each day to each of its main characters, and we have a greater appreciation for the victories of those who survive.

Daddy Was a Number Runner, a growing-up story, belonging to a "skinny and black and bad looking [young girl] with. . . short hair and

209

[a] long neck and all that naked space in between'' (14), also belongs to all of the people who make up Francie's world—all of the men and women and children who love and hate each other, who quarrel and fight among themselves, but who are also capable of expressing concern and tenderness for each other at moments when we least expect them to do so. These are people who feel deeply about everything, because for each one, life is a constant struggle against a barrage of circumstances that threaten to destroy all of their humanity. Like James Baldwin's *Go Tell It on the Mountain* (1952), and Claude Brown's *Manchild in the Promised Land* (1965), this narrative is the personal side of the story of living and growing up feeling entrapped by race and class in the black urban ghetto between the two great wars. And in addition to the limitations placed on the male protagonists in Baldwin's and Brown's books, the heroine of *Daddy Was a Number Runner* must cope with the problems that her gender raises. These three works, reflecting the unquantifiable side of human experiences, are riddled with contradictions and ambiguities, and tell the stories that only poets and artists have been sufficiently gifted to manifest from the beginning of human time.

To begin, Louise Meriwether's central character develops within a context of multilayered social circumstances that often baffle her. If by the end of the novel she seems not to have completely caught up with the worldly wisdom displayed by a number of her friends and acquaintances, it is not for want of experiences toward that end. For the goal of the author is not to have her protagonist make a quantum leap from innocence to full comprehension of the nature of her world in one year, but rather to help readers better understand the complexities of the world of this book and of the metaphoric implications of its title. To achieve this goal, Meriwether has brilliantly created a character in whom we can identify at least two contrasting sides. On one hand, Francie embodies a refreshing and believable naiveté that remains with her throughout; on the other, she also has many of the instincts that we soon recognize as ghetto-survival "smarts." This duality in the protagonist, which is never implausible, gives Francie the unself-conscious narrative ability that initiates readers into the life of depression-bound Harlem. Simultaneously, the double vision we have of Francie reflects a similar ambiguity in the community's responses to its situation. How, we may ask, can the people in this neighborhood, who often evidence a remarkably astute political understanding of the difficulties facing them and all blacks in white America, still maintain such an implicit faith in the fantasy of individual and communal economic revitalization through the numbers? The sheer futility of this collective dream belies the internal strength and sophistication of a people who survived American slavery and beyond. On another level, the numbers game, as metaphor of this particular human situation, constantly reminds us of how tenuous the wellbeing of black American life has always been, and the extent to which the oppression of race, class, and gender influences the aspirations, hopes, and expectations of this entire group of people. It is a theme that pervades the book.

In the summer of 1934, Francie Coffin is twelve years old. She is old enough to know how to use the "jumper" to turn on the electric lights at night (a necessary skill, since months earlier the utility company disconnected the power to their apartment because of nonpayment of bills), and she knows how to sneak a ride on the subway to save a nickel. She is also old enough to know exactly how to hide the numbers slips on the drawer ledge of the buffet in her apartment so that they will not be discovered by the police who periodically take it into their heads to search poor blacks for these scraps ("don't need no warrant," says one to a challenge as he and his partner go about the job of ransacking Francie's apartment). Francie's knowledge is ghetto-survival wisdom, second nature in a jungle where life must lay claim to a minimum of normalcy whether the light bill is paid or not, and where law and order and the policeman's badge (whatever his color may be) is a symbol of the white oppression of black people. Upset by the scene of her father's arrest for his involvement in the numbers racket, her loud crying brings his swift rebuke: " 'Hush,' Daddy said. 'You're a big girl now and you know what to do' ''(74). What she "knows" to do in this situation is that as soon as the police take her father away she will bring the slips downstairs to the contact person and report his arrest. The white overlords in the syndicate will tend to his release.

As far as this novel is concerned, everyone in Harlem plays the numbers, even children like Francie, and there are enough people who make small winnings to keep the hope for a large "hit" alive in everyone's heart. Periodically, someone's number "comes in" for a few hundred dollars, and hope grows stronger. We are better able to comprehend the fragile nature of that hope when we realize that the most popular inspiration for choosing numbers to bet on each day comes from people finding clues in their dreams of the previous night. "I dreamed about fish last night," says Mrs. Mackey, a regular Coffin customer, when Francie comes to collect her bet. "What number does Madame Zora's dream book give for fish?" she asks (13). In this case, the answer is five fourteen, and Mrs. Mackey plays it for twenty-five cents straight, and puts another sixty cents on it in combination. Francie's dreams lead her to make more hits than the other members of her family, and she is very proud of this gift of good luck. No one, including the children, is unaware of the illegality of his or her actions in playing the numbers, or of the inconsistency in the law that permits gambling at the racetrack but not in local neighborhoods. "I can't see the difference between betting at the races or in Harlem," Francie's father complains, "Either gambling's a crime or it ain't" (128). Expectations of winning a huge amount of money by playing the numbers indeed hold the dream of hope that the entire community shares. Adam Coffin expresses the depth of that hope for himself and his neighbors when, in the face of his wife's articulations of her enormous fears of economic chaos, and her anger at him for squandering their few remaining pennies on the game, he explains: "All I'm trying to do is hit a big one again. . . . We almost had us twelve hundred dollars, baby. That's all I'm trying to do. Hit us a big one" (76). This ephemeral hope, which has to renew itself each day, is all that is left for these unemployed black city masses, although they know that, like everything else in Harlem in which money plays an important role, the numbers game is controlled by strong outside forces. Their small winnings do not compare with what is being made off of them each day by the syndicate downtown. "Daddy said the gangsters controlled everything in Harlem," Francie tells us, "the numbers, the whores, and the pimps who brought them their white trade" (22).

In the summer of 1934, Harlem, like the rest of the country, was in the grip of the depression. As the novel shows, men, out of work, congregate in ''knots'' on the sweltering streets, ''doping'' out their numbers, always hoping to beat the odds. The women, needing more than hope to keep their families alive, take the subway to Grand Concourse in the Bronx, where at a prearranged place, on a different sidewalk, they wait for white suburban women who drive up and offer them a pittance for heavy housework. For some of the husbands, like Adam Coffin, the degree to which this action on the part of their wives represents black male failure and humiliation makes it the final blow to their sense of dignity and manhood. They cannot tolerate its symbolic meaning for black survival. And the women, with no options, realize that their efforts to keep body and soul together drive a deeper wedge of unhappiness between themselves and their men, threatening the foundations of their marriages. It is a struggle waged between proud selfhood and starvation.

In the beginning, Francie admires her father because he is different from the men who hang out on the corner all day. When the novel opens, through her eyes, we see him as a man of action, not a victim of hopelessness. Although out of work, he has not given up on life, and she loves him for the tenacity with which he holds on to his pride as a man. Over the course of the year, as the narrative progresses, there is a steady erosion of his will, and in time he struggles less against the forces seeking to overwhelm him. Toward the end of this period, with his fierce pride having been humbled, and his family disintegrating, Francie finds his leaving home to live with Mrs. Mackey less than admirable, and she turns her back on him. It is an act that symbolizes not only the changes going on inside of her, but also her growing awareness of the pitfall of absolute hero worship. ''[I] turned around and watched Daddy trudging down the avenue. Somehow, he didn't seem as big as he used to,'' she notes (203).

Before the breakdown in family stability, however, at home, James Adam Coffin desperately tries to calm his wife's financial anxieties, and for a long time he refuses to permit her to travel to the Bronx to seek out day work, or to agree that his family should go on welfare. Until this long stretch of unemployment, he has been a good financial provider, and his pride in himself is severely threatened by the present circumstances. To save his pride, as conditions worsen, he views all charity with anathema. He even refuses to accept a second-hand couch from Mr. Lipschwitz, the white plumber, who over the years has periodically given the Coffin family his discarded furniture. Adam Coffin plays poker with his friends to occupy part of his time, but on many evenings he gathers his children around him and instead, plays the old piano, an earlier gift from Mr. Lipschwitz. The children know he likes to think he is a virtuoso with the talents of Fats Waller, and they enjoy reinforcing his ego. He tells them stories of his proud royal African ancestress, Yoruba, their great-great grandmother, and of his heroic grandfather, their great-great grandfather, a runaway slave who lived on wild berries in the swamps for seven years. On weekends he plays the piano for rent parties, and occasionally makes a few dollars at that, but most of the time, to his wife's consternation, there is no money with which to pay him. Still, he sees the activity in a positive light for himself. He whips his elder son with violence born out of his frustration from not knowing how to dissuade this first-born from joining a street gang. A man of strong spontaneous emotions, he "shouted and cursed when he was mad, and danced around and hugged you when he was feeling good," Francie reports (17). As a number runner, he enjoys a good reputation for his trustworthiness. Each day he collects the bets and the small sums his neighbors squeeze out to purchase hope, and when someone makes a hit, he pays off promptly. He is like Santa Claus, his daughter surmises, and when someone's number comes in, it is like Christmas.

Against this background of strong moral fiber in the protagonist's father, far from painting a romanticized picture of the squalor of the ghetto, the physical landscape of Louise Meriwether's black Harlem presents a somber image. Francie's Fifth Avenue is, in its dissimilarity to the other, a thousand miles removed from New York City's most fashionable promenade. Roughly fifty blocks removed from the wealth and glitter of the illustrious thoroughfare, this is black Harlem, beginning at approximately 110th Street and moving northward. In the rat-and-bedbug-infested railroad flat in which Francie and her mother, Henrietta, her father, James Adam, and her two older brothers, James Adam, Jr. and Sterling live, the halls are "funky" with the smells of

214

stale food and vomit and urine and a dead rat somewhere down in the basement "bumping together." In the gloom of the overcrowded buildings that stand too close to each other, one must live on the top floor to "snatch a little sunshine," Adam Coffin insists. Outside, on the sidewalks, where most of the living takes place in the summertime, the situation is not better. Here, the foul odors from the overflowing garbage cans on the curb rise to join with those of droppings from the horse-drawn vegetable carts in the street. What saves the day for us, as readers, is the manner in which Francie takes it all in stride, and pulls us quickly along with her. Without apology, she leads us into her world where pimps periodically get killed by the prostitutes they manage, and where black nationalists, anxious parents, and naive youngsters share the same turf. Strange bonds of sympathy unite unlikely groups, and for most of the time, they live and let live.

For all of its negative aspects, Francie's black Harlem has qualities that demonstrate the power of human kindness. It is still a place where a down-and-out borrower can ungrudgingly have a slice of bread or a cup of sugar from the next-door neighbor, if that neighbor is so blessed; and where, as in other ethnic neighborhoods, funerals are rituals in which everyone participates, not only for mourning, but also for another chance to affirm each other and their shared values. "Mr. Caldwell's wake. . .had been nice, all the neighbors bringing in food and wine. The only time it was real sad was at the cemetery when Mrs. Caldwell started wailing" (138), Francie tells us. In this community, where starvation lurks at every door, we note too that there is little selfish hoarding. When Henrietta and Adam Coffin hit their numbers at the same time and come up with a sum that enables them to fend the wolf from the door for a few weeks, the neighbors join in the celebration. We are told that "Daddy had bought two quarts of vanilla and strawberry [ice cream] for us [the children] and a big crock of King Kong [bootleg liquor] for the grownups, though he didn't drink himself" (67). Nor is Meriwether's depiction of the scene devoid of the humor inherent in small details. To the children's chagrin, "most of the women were eating up our cake" (67). As Francie takes us through her world we realize that through her eyes we see more than she knows she sees, not so much because we are outside looking in, but because she is innocently unaware of the depth of her own vision.

The most important consideration for anyone, including a twelve-year-old girl growing up in this environment, is survival, in all of its aspects. How to physically protect the self is a lesson that Francie must learn, and it will provide the model for the way in which she will come to grips with her world. Sukie, one of her best friends, a year older, more street-knowing, "much bigger" than herself, and given to frequent moods of feeling "evil," takes perverse pleasure in often beating up the younger, smaller girl. For a long time Francie's only defense against this treatment is to avoid her friend whenever she suspects the latter is in an "evil mood." This tactic proves ineffective, for sooner or later she always ends up with the beating she sought to avoid. Henrietta Coffin does not interfere in the conflicts between the girls, but she passes on to her daughter the weapon that provides the solution to her plight: the wisdom of knowing that running away from struggle because one is afraid will never resolve the problem. "Francie," she tells the little girl, "you can beat anything, anybody, if you face up to it and if you're not scared" (42). The first time Francie challenges her friend to a fight, Sukie, sensing the changed demeanor in her (now) assailant, declines the opportunity to once again "show off" her superior skills in combat. Nor do the two friends ever fight again.

Another feature of survival that Meriwether stresses here is group cooperation. Individualism is a luxury no one can afford, for staying alive from one day to the next, physically and emotionally, depends on everyone's helping and being helped by others. Mothers share food they have very little of with the most indigent among them; they exchange recipes with each other in search of ways to make the "relief" food palatable for their families; they freely dispense small fragments of information that might be helpful in trying times; and they cry with each other when misfortune strikes at any one of them. If James Adam Coffin is his daughter's favorite parent when the novel opens, because he is "beautiful" and laughs a lot and never whips her, while Henrietta Coffin is "dumpy" and unattractive, and sometimes whips her, it is nevertheless from her mother and the older girls and women in

AFTERWORD

the community that Francie learns those things that are important to her growing up. And it is her mother who remains, even when the family breaks apart, and who stubbornly refuses to succumb to the despair that threatens to swallow up all of her dreams for her children.

Although the particular section of Harlem that Meriwether depicts is confined to a few square blocks, it is typical of the whole in the diverse makeup of the people who live there. In this city within a city, the cultural time is the post-Renaissance, the decade after the flowering of black art and culture in the 1920s when such luminaries as Langston Hughes, Jean Toomer, and Zora Neale Hurston, among the writers, and a great many artists, musicians, and others with aesthetic interests held sway in that "other time when black was beautiful." Francie was born during the Renaissance, but in Brooklyn, and not in the black community. By the time she arrives in Harlem the depression has already changed the face of black-celebration-of-self to one of black-struggle-to-survive. In the 1920s large numbers of black people migrated from rural areas to New York City, among other urban centers, in search of jobs and a better life for themselves and their families. They represented wide variations in color, class, and accent. There were the middle-class intellectuals and the many different artists, attracting each other and attempting to define the positive nature of the black heritage for black and white people; and there were the poor and unlettered rural people, unaware of the significance of their presence in that place at that time, in search of the "promised land." In addition, West Indians and Africans with their lilting voices swelled the numbers, and for a short while, the hope they all felt intimated better times ahead. These immigrants to the cities, native and foreign born, had hoped, as generations of American immigrants before them had done, to improve their living conditions and to make the lives of their children better than their own. Instead, the depression, beginning in 1929, brought them unemployment, poverty, slum housing, crime, a poignant sense of communal powerlessness, and despair. This is Francie's world. In Brooklyn, her father had worked as the janitor in the building in which they lived, in a Jewish neighborhood, where they were the only black people on the block. A painter by trade, he moved his family to Harlem when he was offered a better job in that

217

trade. The hopes they carried with them across the bridge were lost to the depression.

Located at the center of the novel, the trials of the Coffin family, in this pivotal year in the growth and development of their only daughter, provide a paradigm for the fate of many poor black families during the Great Depression. For the men, there is no work, and "hanging out" on the street corner becomes a way of life. The women, knowing that only the irregular demeaning domestic work offered by suburban white housewives, and the even more demeaning attitudes of welfare officials stand between their families' impoverishment and utter destitution, accept their reality with grim fortitude. They take the insults of the case workers along with welfare assistance, and they do domestic work whenever it is available. There are painful resonances between the Grand Concourse rendezvous where white employers and black employees meet and the auction block of slavery times, when black women stood stripped to their waists so that prospective buyers could feast their eyes on the shame of the women's naked femaleness. Here in New York City, the black women at Grand Concourse must have felt psychologically nude, revealing the depth of their predicament in pleading for work that so flagrantly exploited their labor. They must have felt ashamed to be so needy. Francie relates her mother's experiences on her first day on that "block."

> She told me later that she waited on the sidewalk under an awning with the other colored women. When a white lady drove up and asked how much she charged by the hour, Mother said thirty-five cents and was hired for three half days a week by a Mrs. Schwartz. (47)

It is little wonder that China Doll, the older sister of Francie's friend Sukie, chooses a different kind of profession, which in her reasoning, allows her a small way to fight back.

> China Doll was nice.... [She] often gave us a dime if she had it.... Once she told us that hustling was just a job to her, better than breaking her back like her mother did [on housework] for pennies a day. She said ofays were gonna get you one way

or the other so you might as well make them pay for it and try to give them a dose of clap in the bargain. (120)

In spite of her "work," China Doll has important principles of her own, and she is firm with the younger girls to "go and get [their] schooling." She is not unaware of the undesirability of her way of life—it is the absence of options and her greater antipathy to what she considers the more oppressive nature of other things open to her that dictate her choice of this work.

The exploitive nature of the domestic work available to black women at the time, and the social denial to them of other opportunities for gainful employment based on their wishes and abilities, are further explored in the novel. There is the time when Francie's mother is outraged at the way in which her daughter is treated on her first venture into paid work. Having agreed to accept a dollar for "just a little dusting and washing dishes and things like that for maybe five hours," from Mrs. Rathbone and her daughter Rachel, the wife and daughter of the white candystore owner, Francie discovers she is also expected to scrub kitchen floors, sweep the carpets, and wash tenth floor windows from the outside by sitting on the ledges. On learning this, Henrietta Coffin explodes in anger at the storekeeper (although he is innocent of the matter) and assures her child:

> You don't have to do no domestic work for nobody, Francie. . . . You don't be no fool, you hear? You finish school and go on to college. Long as I live you don't have to scrub no white folks' floors or wash their filthy windows. What they think I'm spending my life on my knees in their kitchens for? So you can follow in my footsteps? You finish school and go on to college. Somebody in this family got to finish school. (191-92)

Louise Meriwether is not the only black woman writer to address the problems of the black domestic worker in fiction. The earliest black novel of which we know, Harriet Wilson's *Our Nig; or Sketches from the Life of a Free Black in a Two-Story White House, North, Showing That Slavery's Shadows Fall Even There,* published in 1859, details the horrendous treatment that a young black orphaned girl receives during the time that she spends as a domestic drudge in the home of white caretakers. So badly is she treated in terms of the quantity and difficulty of the work, the poor food she receives and the curtailment of her rest time, that by the time she is eighteen years old and free to go into the world on her own, her health is irreparably damaged for the rest of her life. In a state in which slavery had long been abolished, this child was treated no less shamefully by the woman of the house than the most abused slave in the South. Ann Petry's *The Street* (1946), Alice Childress's *Like One of the Family: Conversations from a Domestic's Life* (1956), Paule Marshall's *Brown Girls, Brownstones* (1959), and Toni Morrison's *The Bluest Eye* (1972) also probe the difficulties that black women encounter in their relationships with white women who employ them to work in their homes. Marshall's West Indian women have a profound psychological understanding of their relationship to middle-class white women and the "few raw mouth pennies" they earn each day; Childress's protagonist is satiric in her attitudes toward her employers, and even succeeds in facing them down on occasion; Morrison's Pauline has no respect for her superficial mistress. In every instance, the conditions of employment are so designed that only the strongest black women survive with dignity in the face of the insults they must absorb in carrying out their tasks. Henrietta Coffin is sufficiently sure of her own self-worth and pragmatic enough in her approach to the hardships of her life to have earned a place in this group. But for poor working-class black women, and even some with trade skills, only this menial work or prostitution, outside of the law, was open to them for a long time.

The denial of work choices to black women, which begins while they are girls, is further emphasized by Meriwether in a school incident in this novel. In comparison to the majority of her friends who are often left behind at the end of each school year, Francie does well in her academic subjects, but hates cooking and sewing, which she is also made to take. When she turns in a completed cookbook and a finished dress, neither of them her own work, she receives compliments from her teachers. "You might make a good seamstress one day, that's a good living, you know," the white sewing teacher tells her. Francie protests this narrowing of her horizon, and insists that she wants to be a secretary when she grows up. Just as other white racist teachers have disallowed the ambitions of millions of black boys and girls in America, Francie's teacher points out to the little girl that she needs to be "practical" in her expectations, for no jobs for black women exist in the areas of her interest. In school, she is told, she needs to concentrate on the skills she will be able to exercise when she becomes an adult. To herself, the teacher wonders why courses like typing and shorthand are taught in black schools, since they can only cause frustration for students like Francie.

Despite racism of this kind, and many other factors that offer discouragements in this area, from the emancipation from slavery in the nineteenth century until the present time, education has been seen by the majority of black people as the individual's and the group's most dependable and desirable avenue to greater social mobility and economic advancement. As a guiding principle, it is a central issue in this novel. But it is also clear that the children of the black immigrants to the cities are rejecting the faith in education and the philosophy of hope in the American dream that their elders hold. Their measure of the rewards to be gained against the sacrifices these entail speak to their alienation from the older generation.

For the young, the politics of race generates pessimism and skepticism toward the goals and ideals of their parents. Early in his young manhood, James Junior disregards his mother's and father's hopes and plans for his education in spite of the dissension this creates between him and them. Choosing peer-group approval instead, he joins a street gang, and resigns himself to the beatings his father gives him for his open defiance. This action proves to be a mistake on his part, and later gets him into serious trouble with the law. The generation of the elder Coffins had asked only for an opportunity to do regular honest work for a living wage; to live modestly but decently; and to have the chance to prepare their children to take advantage of some of the social options that other Americans enjoy. Their children, by the time they become teenagers, have other ideas. They are too impatient to assume the tedious struggle against racism in a manner that yields only small, if any, personal gains, and they want to have immediate access to the "good" life, which, in their estimation, money easily procures. And they have also learned that there are other ways to get money than by hard, honest work. They choose different heroes and different goals from their fathers and mothers.

In the ultimate break with his parents' wishes, James Junior chooses the "glamour" of the life of the pimp instead, with its promise of a regular supply of brand-new suits, suede shoes, diamond rings, a big car, and plenty of money. For a time, the Coffins see their younger boy, Sterling, who has a strong interest in science and experiments, as their "salvation," fulfilling their wishes for upward mobility through education and a professional life. They are confident that he will complete high school and continue on to college. Once again, however, their hopes end in disappointment. After a couple of years Sterling too grows tired of the poverty that makes him look like a "ragpicker" among the more affluent white students in his school outside of the black ghetto; of the "peanuts" he earns from shining shoes on weekends; and of anticipating the hardships he will face securing employment as a black chemist after spending years in college to learn that trade. Not wanting to confront the uncertainty of his fate through education, he gives up his ambitions to take a job with an undertaker for seven dollars a week. Our sympathies go out to Adam Coffin when he vents the depth of his disappointment and his inability to productively direct the lives of his children: "I would have gotten the money somehow, . . . I swear. I would have stolen the money if need be to get Sterling in college" (172). It is a cry of great pain. Henrietta Coffin assuages her disappointment in her sons by shifting the burden of her expectations onto the shoulders of her daughter, and once more utters the parental willingness to make the utmost sacrifice to enable a child of hers to have the advantages of a college education. Francie need not have to scrub white people's floors.

While the larger emphasis in the novel is on the effects of the depression on the lives of the people within the black community, and on the changes in attitude toward black life in general by the first large urban-born generation of the group, Meriwether also treats the impact of outsiders on the lives of Harlemites at this time, and the effects of black crime on black families. Unlike most narratives that explore black/white interactions by looking at the ways in which blacks are treated in white settings, this novel also examines how whites who come into Harlem affect the lives of its inhabitants. Here, only black women who are domestics have contact with whites outside of Harlem, and this is reported on, not observed by readers. Two things stand out in the depiction of the influence of whites within the black community: the prevalence of sexual molestation of little girls by white men, and the economic drain on the community that results from the debilitating practices of white landlords and merchants.

More than a decade after the publication of *Daddy Was a Number Runner*, Audre Lorde, in her "biomythography" *Zami: A New Spelling of My Name* (1982), would also address the issue of the sexual molestation of little girls in Harlem by white storekeepers and others like them who frequented Harlem during the daytime in the 1920s and 1930s. There is no reason to reiterate here the long history of sexual power that white men have exercised over black women's lives since the days of slavery. However, in the narratives of Lorde and Meriwether, one a fictionalized autobiography, the other, a novel with autobiographical elements, we become aware that neither the perverse attraction some white men have had for black women, nor the desire and the opportunity to carry out their fantasies were eliminated with the emancipation proclamation or the movement from plantation to city ghetto.

As Francie tells her story we discover how early little black girls must learn to protect themselves from this abuse, and the extent to which the men—respectable tradesmen like the butcher and the baker, or the less visible men who make it their business to go into dark movie houses at the hours when unattended children are most likely to be there, or those who expose themselves for lewd purposes on rooftops or in parks—prey on the innocence of these children. Why the girls do not tell their parents of these encounters is the immediate question that comes to mind. No definitive answers are easily forthcoming, but at least partial explanations include the girls' fear of the violence that might follow; their fear that they might not be believed, and instead, be perceived as having "evil" minds, especially in the cases involving the tradesmen; or their inability to articulate the circumstances without feeling somehow responsible for the actions of the men. One thing is clear—these children receive no sex education from mothers or older sisters. This is demonstrated when Francie has her first menstrual period. "Francie, this means you're growing up," her mother says, trying to calm her daughter's anxieties over the sudden appearance of blood in her bloomers. The child waits for more—for an explanation—but all she receives is an injunction to change the soiled pad every couple of hours, and "don't let no boys mess around with you." Francie comments: "Then she was gone, but I didn't understand any more about the period now than I had before, and what did messing around with boys have to do with it" (80)?

The inadequate preparation for handling the development of their sexuality, in conjunction with the kind of street knowledge girls like Francie acquire at a very early age, inevitably affect their ability to bring the problems they encounter with the men to their elders. What they do, however, is to attempt to take some control of the behavior they do not welcome. Invited by the man on her roof (who also follows her into the movies, and who is later murdered by some of the members of her brother's gang) to come up and touch his exposed penis, Francie tells him to throw down the dime he promised he would give her if she did what he asked. As soon as he does so she disappears inside her apartment without granting his wish. On another occasion Francie and Sukie, together in the park, receive a nickel each from an old white man who wants to take a look at their genitals. They succeed in granting him the merest glimpse of their private parts. "I was glad Sukie never let any of these bums touch us," Francie comments on this occasion. "It was bad enough having the butcher and Max the Baker always sneaking a feel, but at least they were clean" (45): In the close confines of the butcher or baker shop, Francie finds it harder to avoid the "feeling up" these men do to her every chance they get, but still does what she can to escape their preying hands. Liberation from this harrassment comes for her during the summer of her thirteenth year when she takes direct action to end it. Not surprisingly, this occurs at a time when she is feeling that "Harlem was nothing but one big garbage heap" (174). In sheer frustration with the conditions she sees—the crowded streets with garbage strewn over them, the disappointments in her family, the hopelessness most people are feeling—she brings up her knee and aims it between the legs of Max the Baker as he offers her a bag of stale cookies and tries to slide his hand across her breasts. We know that she will free herself of this harrassment because she promises herself that on the morrow she will "get" the butcher in the same way. As her body begins its transformation from child to woman, in spite of the gaps in her sexual education, she will be able to protect herself from the unwanted attentions of those who had previously been able to take advantage of her innocence.

A good deal has been debated and written in recent times in regard to black/Jewish American relationships. Antagonism and mutual sympathies, differences and similarities between the two groups have been explored and questioned on a variety of levels. With two exceptions, Meriwether's book, in which most of the whites who interact with blacks are Jewish, does not give us a positive reading of these relationships in day-to-day Harlem life during this historical period. There are no opportunities for the two groups to meet as equals, and in addition to the sexual harrassment issue and the negative teacher-student encounters, the adults of the groups meet each other only on two levels: one, in the relationship between tenants and landlords or customers and storekeepers; the other, as domestic workers and their women employers. In both cases black people appear victimized and exploited. The two white people who do not project negative attitudes toward Harlem's black residents are Mr. Rathbone, who owns the candy store and is often kind to Francie without ever molesting her, and Mr. Lipschwitz, the plumber, who is generous to the Coffins with the furniture his family no longer needs. He also maintains his dignity with the young girls. At the same time, Mrs. Rathbone expects Francie to do much harder work than someone her age should do.

When Harlem became predominantly black, in the early part of this century, the Jewish people who had previously been the majority living there moved to the suburbs. However, as the novel illustrates, many proceeded to hold on to city real estate and became absentee landlords, while others continued to maintain their businesses within the black community. Black tenant overcrowding, joblessness, and lack of respect for the property of others, as well as the racism of white landlords wishing to make huge profits with a minimum of investment are all blamed for the animosities between the landlords and tenants. Nonresident merchants trading in Harlem with no sense of responsibility to that place charge exhorbitant prices for inferior commodities, and cause an economic drain of profits out of the community. The racism of white Jewish women is indicated in their exploitation of the misfortunes of black women who have no alternative but to seek domestic employment from them. Still, the black reactions that emanate from these situations do not in themselves constitute a universal disapproval of Jews as a group, but rather an active dislike of those with whom black Harlem comes into contact—landlords, small storekeepers, teachers who stifle ambitions, and domestic employers. Within the general context of race and class in American society, the minority ethnic and racial search for upward mobility, and the pressures of the depression, it is not surprising that the black people in this book should feel as they do toward those white people with whom they come into contact. That the majority of these are Jews reflects the historical pattern of ethnic migration to and from the city.

One of the most moving subplots within this novel deals with the way in which crime was beginning to affect black families in Harlem in the 1930s. In fact, the events delineated here demand that the reader attempt to understand the disastrous impact of race and class prejudice on human behavior, and to recognize how unmeasurable is the waste and suffering these cause, not only to blacks, but also to whites. The West Indian Caldwells, the family severely affected, are immigrants in search of a better life for their children. Far from being irresponsible parents, Mr. Caldwell, we are told, "was awfully strict with them, but he loved his boys." Mrs. Caldwell does her best to establish a compromise between a demanding father and his strong-willed sons, and to keep them from following undesirable paths. Both parents and children, however, find their lives tragically entangled with urban crime, and Mr. Caldwell dies of pneumonia. The pathos in the portrayal of the fate of the two sons raises many disquieting questions for us. How, for instance, do we react to Mrs. Caldwell's heartrending cry when she learns of her younger son's conviction for murder: "It took me sixteen years to raise that boy . . . . How could a handful of people decide in two hours that he ain't fit to live" (155)?

When these lines accost our "priviledged" eyes, what do we actually hear in the words of the poor-but-law-abiding widow and welfare mother, who even before this final catastrophe was hard pressed to cope with the reality of one son for whom jail was already a "second home"? Do we question the existence of a relationship between Mr. Caldwell's death and his two sons taking "to the streets like wild animals?" Do we consider the possibility that the father may have died because he forced his physical strength beyond its boundary in a determined effort to overcome his economic deprivation? West Indians, we know, have been wont to believe that black Americans would be socially and economically better off if they only worked harder. Is it possible that the Caldwell sons rebelled against that ethic because they perceived only futility in their father's life of work, no matter how hard he willed it otherwise? Mrs. Caldwell mourns because, in spite of everything she had done to raise her sons "right," she has failed. Do we question the justice that sets a mobster boss free because he is able to "[pay] off the jury," but which then sends poor young black boys to die even though everyone, including the judge who sentenced them, knows that their "confessions" were beaten out of them?

How do we understand the pain of the black mother and still find sympathy for the survivors of the crime, the young white widow and her two little girls? To them, the murdered man was the husband and father they loved, the stable provider in their well-ordered family. They know only that he was brutally and senselessly killed. They do not know of the hidden side of his respectable life: his offences of child molestation in dark movie houses and on Harlem rooftops, and his penchant for regularly visiting a black prostitute. But are these actions sufficient for us to justify or even pardon the taking of his life? If not, do we concur with the jury (not of their peers) that the three young convicted men-boys are shiftless, irresponsible animals, deserving of the "nothing" they have received from life, even though they live in a world in which everyone, even the losers, know that "a man's got to have something . . . so he knows he's a man" (65)? Or do we see them as victims of a society in which the cards are so stacked against them that their tragic end is inevitable?

There are no tidy answers to the questions raised by the particular events in this book. Neither the myth of Horatio Alger, which categorically condemns those who fail for their lack of initiative, nor the naturalism of Theodore Dreiser, which exonerates failure on the basis of human impotence against the forces of the environment, applies here. If we respond honestly to this text we know that a combination of forces are at work, and that the social realities of class, race, and gender oppression, which are intricately woven into the fabric of this story, make it impossible to impute blame or withhold sympathy through simplistic analysis of the circumstances. If the boys must be held responsible for their actions (and I think they must be), then so should Dutch Schultz, the shoe salesman, and the white men and women who use their privileged status to take advantage of those for whom that privilege is never possible.

One of the strengths of this book is the balance that Meriwether creates in showing positive and negative aspects in the lives of her characters. In spite of the depression, the rise of crime, and the ways in which race, class, and gender impinge on the humanity of black people, there are evidences of another side of the experience. Francie reads fairy tales until she discovers books by and about black people: books like Claude McKay's *Home to Harlem* (1928). Her sense of self is heightened when she discovers that someone has written about the same "raggedy streets" she traverses and the "clowns" on Fifth Avenue who often annoy her. She finds this literature from life "very funny and kind of sad," but it gives her ammunition to use in her own development. Other aspects of Harlem life are also positive. For fifteen cents, we learn, it is possible to have a hearty meal of golden brown chicken, bread, and vegetables at Father Divine's headquarters. A decade after Marcus Garvey had stirred the racial pride of millions of black Americans, his name and his philosophy are still heard on the corners where street speakers hold forth. Henrietta Coffin, born a Methodist, regularly attends Abyssinia Baptist Church, along with thousands of other black people, to hear Adam Clayton Powell expound on white racism, the problems of Haile Selassie, and the terrible lynchings taking place in different parts of the country. Adam Coffin does not go to church, but he admires Powell for having been responsible for the opening of a free food kitchen that fed thousands of starving Harlemites during this difficult period. Activists mobilize sentiments to support the Scottsboro Boys, and when the "Brown Bomber" defeats the "Butcher Boy" all Harlem celebrates:

> Strangers hugged me and I squeezed them back. It was good to feel their touch. . . . The crowd spilled off the pavement into the street, stalling cars, which honked good-naturedly and then gave up as the riders jumped out and joined us lindying down the middle of Lenox Avenue (194).

The misery of the families unable to meet their bills and breaking apart in the wake of an inhuman welfare system, has its opposite dimension in the life of Henrietta Coffin's sister, Francie's Aunt Hazel. Unhampered by husband or children, and holding down a steady live-in domestic job in the suburbs, Aunt Hazel's existence appears carefree in comparison to that of people like the Coffins. On Thursdays, when she is off from work, she stays in her Harlem apartment and entertains her West Indian friend, Mr. Mulberry, a live-in handyman who also has Thursdays off. Francie likes her aunt, who has long hair that she wears in a bun on the top of her head, is always jolly, drinks gin and wine, and smells "nice, like cake baking." She never minds the missions that take her to visit Aunt Hazel ("to borrow money I was never sent to pay back"), and not only for the food (fried-fish sandwiches, cake, and milk), which she always gets when she is there, but also because of her aunt's genuine warmth and the order in her home. In spite of the funky hallways in Aunt Hazel's building, just like all the other hallways in Harlem, her tiny rooms are spotless, and everything is in its place. Her space is "not junky like ours," Francie says. Although only a minor character in the novel, Aunt Hazel's generosity toward her almost destitute family is another indication of the presence of human kindness and family cooperation even in so bleak a landscape.

Daddy Was a Number Runner ends on notes that reinforce the idea that hope continues to live in spite of the failures that have characterized the lives of many American blacks throughout their history. As the narrative moves to its conclusion, there are moments when Francie feels, in spite of all that is wrong with her community, that it is still a place that has value. On a particular Saturday morning soon after her thirteenth birthday, as she watches a group of young boys across the street from her apartment ''acting the fool as usual,'' she has a strong sense of the joy of life in their loud and carefree laughter: ''I wanted to hug them all,'' she tells us. ''We belonged to each other somehow. . . . [T]he sweet feeling hung on and I loved all of Harlem gently and didn't want to be Puerto Rican or anything but my own rusty self'' (184). At other times, when dramatic changes seem impossible, she feels despondent. For instance, the suggestion of her friend Sukie that as adult women ''either you was a whore like China Doll or you worked in a laundry or did day's work or ran poker games or had a baby every year'' (207) depresses her. Borrowing sparingly from Ann Petry's naturalistic novel, *The Street,* in which a poor but ambitious young black woman is destroyed by the malignant Harlem environment, Meriwether has Francie raise the question of whether her Fifth Avenue is a trap of poverty and despair from which she and her family can never escape. From one angle, it looks this way, for in this text, race, class, and gender are powerful obstacles that constantly defy the possibilities of success. But this novel steers a clear path away from the pessimism of naturalism. Significantly, it is Henrietta Coffin, welfare mother and exploited domestic worker, deserted by her husband, with her dreams for her sons having fallen away, and with no tangible proof that her life will ever be better, who is not trapped in the ''coffin'' of her spirit. Her voice echoes the self-confidence of millions like herself who, in the face of dreams deferred, hold on. When her daughter inquires of her if they will ever be free to leave the street, Henrietta Coffin thinks, then responds: ''One of these days, Francie, we gonna move off these mean streets'' (175). Her statement is a celebration of the power of the human spirit.

Daddy Was a Number Runner is a well-crafted work of art that captures the essence of a historical time and place in the experiences of black people, but especially of the extent to which black women suffer, face failures not of their own making, take responsibility for themselves and their families, and sometimes transcend the difficulties of their lives even when their men fail them. Told in the voice of the adolescent narrator, through Francie's eyes, readers have a front-seat view, devoid of moralizing or sensationalism, of how a young girl felt in that place and in that time. Faithful to the idea of the complex nature of experience, Meriwether does not blame the men for their inability to secure work, nor does she castigate them (Adam Coffin, for instance) for their inability to remain stoically with their families through the worst times. Her sympathetic portrayal of the ways in which circumstances beyond their control undermine their pride in themselves is skillfully handled. At the same time, because Meriwether respects the men's humanity, her treatment of them is never condescending and she makes no apologies for them. In the final analysis, she leaves them responsible for their actions without passing moral judgments on their failures.

Finally, this book is largely a tribute to poor, uneducated, black women, who, through centuries of watching their men being ground down by poverty and racism continue to live each day with the assurance that conditions will improve. Expecting little for themselves, not from lack of self-worth, but because they understand the politics of race, gender, economics,and power, they scrub floors, wash windows, and absorb racist and sexist insults, so that their children can have better lives than their own. In the contrast in the portraits of Henrietta Coffin and the other mothers with Aunt Hazel, Meriwether demonstrates how even the family oppresses women. Aunt Hazel escapes the worst aspects of the depression because she has no husband or children, and is free to take advantage of a live-in job, and so to meet her own financial needs. Still, Aunt Hazel's life leaves much to be desired, as stories of live-in domestics attest. (See, for example, Paule Marshall's "Reena" in *Reena and Other Stories*, 1983.) However, in this work, Aunt Hazel's willingness to help her sister and niece and nephews further confirms the existence and importance of the community of women. It is this community that provides the core of strength that sustains the women in this novel: from the willingness to lend a slice of bread or a cup of sugar, to accompanying a distraught mother on a visit to her incarcerated son.

AFTERWORD

Meriwether affirms this community through the voice of Francie Coffin, who we are sure will go to college so that Henrietta Coffin's hope for her children will not have been in vain.

Louise Jenkins Meriwether, the third of five children, was born in Haverstraw, New York, of parents who had moved from South Carolina to New York, by way of Philadelphia, early in this century. They too were members of the twentieth-century black pilgrimage in search of a better life. Like Francie in her novel, Meriwether spent her adolescence in Harlem, and her father, Lloyd Jenkins, a bricklayer by trade, became a number runner when he was unable to find other work during the depression. In spite of the misfortunes of the family, Meriwether graduated from New York University before she married and moved to the Midwest, and later to Los Angeles, with her husband, who was a teacher. However, the marriage did not last, and her second attempt at matrimony shared a similar fate. Although Meriwether earned a master's degree in journalism from the University of California at Los Angeles in 1965, and worked as a reporter for the *Los Angeles Sentinel,* her main concern had always been with establishing herself as a writer. Her first articles appeared in *Negro Digest* and other black journals from the mid to late 1960s; her favorite topic was black men and women who had achieved in spite of difficult circumstances. In the late 1960s she joined the Watts Writers Workshop and contributed to the *Antioch Review* when the group was invited to do so. "Daddy Was a Number Runner" first appeared as a short story in that journal in 1967, and in the following year, another story, "A Happening in Barbados," was also published there.

While working on her novel, Meriwether became involved with a group that opposed Twentieth Century Fox in its effort to produce a film based on William Styron's *The Confessions of Nat Turner,* which many believed presented an inaccurate and distorted view of Turner. Her efforts came to the attention of Martin Luther King, Jr., among other notable civil rights activists of the time. Much to her gratification, the movie was never produced. In the summer of 1965 she was associated with the Congress of Racial Equality (CORE) in Bogalusa,

232

AFTERWORD

Louisiana, as a "gun toter" for a radical group, the Deacons, who were protecting blacks from harrassment by the Ku Klux Klan. Her experiences here provided the basis for her story "The Girl from Creektown" (1972). Since then she has also been vocal against apartheid in South Africa.

Daddy Was a Number Runner, the first novel to come out of the Watts Writing Workshop, was five years in the writing and underwent extensive revisions before its publication in 1970. In its first life it went through twelve printings, with hardcover sales of close to 20,000 copies and paperback sales exceeding 400,000 copies. Favorable critical attention came from many quarters including the *Saturday Review* and black writers Paule Marshall and James Baldwin. With its current publication by The Feminist Press it joins the ranks of feminist classics that will speak to generations to come.

Louise Meriwether returned to New York in the 1970s. Since then she has written three biographies of famous blacks for elementary school children. *The Freedom Ship of Robert Smalls* (1971) is an account of a South Carolina slave who hijacked a Confederate gunboat and reached the Union fleet in safety in 1892. After the emancipation he served five terms as a representative to Congress from his home town of Beaufort, South Carolina. *The Heart Man: Dr. Daniel Hale Williams* (1972) deals with the struggles and successes of the famous nineteenth-century black heart surgeon. Dr. Williams is credited with opening the first hospital (in Chicago in 1891) in which black nurses were trained, and which admitted patients of more than one race. For all of his success, including having been the first person in America to perform heart surgery, he was never allowed to join white professional societies. In 1973 Meriwether published *Don't Ride the Bus on Monday: The Rosa Park Story,* a tribute to the middle-aged black woman whose refusal to give up her seat on a segregated bus in Montgomery, Alabama, sparked the boycott that had enormous repercussions in mobilizing the Civil Rights Movement of the late 1950s and 1960s.

Louise Meriwether now lives in New York City and teaches writing courses at Sarah Lawrence College. She belongs to the Harlem

Writers Guild and has taught a fiction workshop at the Frederick Douglass Creative Arts Center for a number of years. She continues to write and is working on a historical novel about the Civil War and Reconstruction. She has always had, she says, a special interest in and love for history.

Nellie McKay
University of Wisconsin—Madison

LOUISE MERIWETHER is a prominent author, journalist, essayist, and antiwar activist. She is the author of several books, including *Fragments of the Ark* and *Shadow Dancing*, as well as children's biographies of African American icons such as Rosa Parks and Dr. Daniel Hale Williams. She was an early member of the Harlem Writers Guild and the Watts Writers Workshop, and the first black woman to be hired as a story editor in Hollywood. She has taught creative writing at Sarah Lawrence College and the University of Houston, and is a winner of grants from the National Endowment for the Arts, Mellon Foundation, and New York State Council on the Arts. In 2016 she received a lifetime achievement award from the Before Columbus Foundation, and her birthday, May 8, was declared Louise Meriwether Appreciation Day by Manhattan borough president Gale Brewer. To honor her literary legacy, the Feminist Press launched the Louise Meriwether First Book Prize in 2016 to lift up women and nonbinary debut authors of color.

JAMES BALDWIN (1924–1987) was a prolific writer known for his novels on racial and sexual identity, such as the semiautobiographical *Go Tell It on the Mountain* and the pioneering gay novel *Giovanni's Room*. A voice of the civil rights movement, he published several piercing books including *The Fire Next Time* and *No Name in the Street*. Since his passing, both the National James Baldwin Literary Society and Hampshire College's James Baldwin Scholars program have been established in his honor. In 2016 his unfinished manuscript, "Remember This House," was the basis of Raoul Peck's Oscar-nominated documentary *I Am Not Your Negro*.

NELLIE Y. McKAY (1930–2006) was an academic and author best known for coediting *The Norton Anthology of African American Literature*. She was Evjue Professor of American and African American literature in the Afro-American studies department, and held joint appointments in the English and women's studies departments at the University of Wisconsin-Madison. She was instrumental in inserting African American authors into the modern literary canon as well as establishing black women's studies in the academy. Her research interests included nineteenth- and twentieth-century American and African American literatures, black women's writing, and US multiculturalism.

The Feminist Press publishes books that ignite movements and social transformation. Celebrating our legacy, we lift up insurgent and marginalized voices from around the world to build a more just future.

See our complete list of books at
feministpress.org

THE FEMINIST PRESS
AT THE CITY UNIVERSITY OF NEW YORK
FEMINISTPRESS.ORG

Printed in the USA
CPSIA information can be obtained
at www.ICGtesting.com
JSHW080954040124
54795JS00001B/1